'You're not g_____
I'm through _____

'Until you're th____
asked, glaring up at Antonio. 'Just who do you
think you are?'

'Someone you should be afraid of, someone
who isn't about to be taken in by those big eyes
and reassuring bedside manner which, I
suspect, you've been laying on thick ever since
you set foot into this house!'

**Dear Reader**

The nights are drawing in again . . . the perfect excuse for snuggling up with a Mills & Boon romance! November is the time for bonfires and fireworks, of course—and you'll find plenty of sparks flying between the heroes and heroines in this month's collection of love stories! Look out for books by some of your favourite authors . . . and, if you're missing the summer sun, why not let us transport you to sunny California and exotic Mexico? So shut out the winter darkness, and enter the warm and wonderful world of Mills & Boon!

*The Editor*

**Cathy Williams** is Trinidadian and was brought up on the twin islands of Trinidad and Tobago. She was awarded a scholarship to study in Britain, and came to Exeter University in 1975 to continue her studies into the great loves of her life: languages and literature. It was there that Cathy met her husband, Richard. Since they married Cathy has lived in England, originally in the Thames Valley but now in the Midlands. Cathy and Richard have two small daughters.

**Recent titles by the same author:**

UNWILLING SURRENDER
SHADOWS OF YESTERDAY

# A THORN
# IN PARADISE

BY
## CATHY WILLIAMS

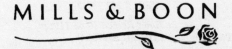

# MILLS & BOON

## MILLS & BOON LIMITED
ETON HOUSE, 18-24 PARADISE ROAD
RICHMOND, SURREY TW9 1SR

*MILLS & BOON and the Rose Device
are trademarks of the publisher.*

*First published in Great Britain 1994
by Mills & Boon Limited*

© Cathy Williams 1994

*Australian copyright 1994   Philippine copyright 1994
This edition 1994*

ISBN 0 263 78743 5

*Set in Times Roman 10 on 11½ pt.
01-9411-54766 C*

*Made and printed in Great Britain*

# CHAPTER ONE

THE grounds of Deanbridge House were magnificent. They stretched in front of Corinna, well groomed, tended as they were by countless gardeners and, in the bloom of summer, ablaze with flowers, yellow, purple, red, perfectly manicured splashes of colour which were the backdrop to the rows of trees on either side, and beyond which lay yet more grounds, all similarly impeccable, and interspersed with stone benches and fountains.

After nine months, she still continued to be amazed and delighted by the sheer magnificence of the place. It wasn't simply the size of the house and estate, but the fact that absolutely nothing about either jarred. Everything contained within those acres of land was pleasing to the eye.

Benjamin Silver, though, was not so enamoured of the vista and Corinna had long concluded that a lifetime surrounded by such beauty had jaded his palate.

Right now he was ranting on about his son, from whom he had unexpectedly received a letter, and she half listened to what he was saying, not taking in a great deal because, after all this time working for him, she knew almost as much about his son as she did about herself, and none of it was very pleasant.

'Who the hell does he think he is?' the old man was grumbling from his wheelchair. 'Nothing from him in years, not a letter, not so much as a Christmas card, then all of a sudden he's writing to inform me—*inform me, mind*!—that he's thinking of coming across! Who does he think he is? Answer me that!'

Corinna smiled down at the silver head, and he roared from his wheelchair, 'And you can wipe that smile off your face!'

'How did you know I was smiling?' she asked and, if he was capable of turning around to glare at her, she knew that he would have, but age had rusted his limbs, even though he was only seventy.

'Stop trying to change the subject!'

'I wasn't,' she protested, pushing along the wheelchair to their favourite spot by one of the fountains. 'It's such a beautiful morning, though; why spoil it by being annoyed?' She reached the bench by the fountain and stopped, sitting down and lifting her face to the sun.

She was a tall, slender girl with the sort of fair complexion that didn't tan at all. Usually she wore a wide brimmed straw hat for these mid-morning walks, but today she had forgotten and it was lovely to feel the warmth on her face, even though she might go pink from it. Her waist-length fair hair had been braided into a single plait which hung over the back of the bench.

'And spin me round to face you. I don't care to be talking to a damned fountain!'

She obeyed and eyed him with amusement. When she had first come to work for Benjamin Silver, she had been warned by the agency that there was a good chance that she wouldn't last a week.

'None of our nurses has stayed on,' she had been informed. 'They might like the surroundings, Deanbridge House is a spectacular place, but old Ben Silver is a cantankerous so-and-so. He can be downright rude when it suits him, which is most of the time, and they can't put up with it.'

Corinna had very quickly sized up the situation. Benjamin Silver was a lonely old man. His only child, a son, had fallen out with him years ago, and most of his relatives were dead.

'The rest,' he had told her, 'might just as well be.'

It had only been her sympathy for him, and her sense of humour, which had allowed her to survive his blasts of temper, and now they had become accustomed to each other. She loved him and she knew that he was fond of her, for all his occasional rages.

'I won't see him!' he was telling her, his blue eyes fierce. 'I won't let him so much as set one foot through that door. I'll set the dogs on him.'

'I'm sure he'll be scared stiff,' she said from her reclining position on the bench. 'Being confronted by two toothless, watery-eyed Labradors will really make him quake with fear.'

'I should have got rid of those good-for-nothing hounds years ago,' he muttered. 'I was a sentimental old fool, and now that I need a couple of vicious animals, I'm paying for that bit of short-sightedness. Well, I'll set Edna on him.'

'That's more like it,' Corinna said, her full lips curving into a smile. Edna was the chief housekeeper and could be a dragon when it suited her. She was far more ferocious than the dogs.

He grinned reluctantly. 'You're not taking me seriously. We should be getting back. This sun's no good for you. You'll end up looking like a lobster.'

'You're such a charmer,' she said, standing up and pushing him back towards the house. 'Are you sure your son doesn't take after you more than you'd like to think?'

'Don't be impertinent, young lady,' Benjamin roared. 'He's nothing like me! Not that I can remember anyway. It's been so long since I last clapped eyes on him that anybody could walk off the street and call himself my son and I'd be none the wiser.'

This, Corinna realised, was nearer the truth than might be expected.

Whatever had caused the feud between father and son, and in all his rantings Benjamin had never disclosed, it was a bitter one. There were no pictures of his son anywhere that she had ever seen. She had no idea whether he was short, tall, fat, thin, fair-haired or dark-haired. She had built her own mental picture of him, though. A man in his mid-forties, fattish because he was successful and successful men never seemed able to resist the lure of good food and fine wine. Possibly he was arrogant—that at any rate was what she had been told in great detail—but equally possible was that he was now no more than a tired, overworked businessman who had been too proud to revisit the family home. Who knew? He might even be married with twelve children. Benjamin had never volunteered the information and she had not pried. She knew from her own experience how irritating and uncomfortable other people's curiosity could be. She could remember, from all those years ago, the greedy nosiness of some of her so-called friends as they tried to elicit the details of her private misfortune. They had called it concern, but she had recognised it for what it was, the feeding of vultures on someone else's grief.

He was still venting his anger when she settled him into bed at nine that night.

He had carried the letter around with him for the entire day, and the last thing he had done before she had left his bedroom was to pull it out and wave it in her face, with a scowl.

'I shouldn't be subjected to this at my age!' he told her. 'I should be taking things easy, not getting worked up like this. You know that. You nag me often enough about my blood-pressure.'

'Yes,' Corinna said, perching on the side of his bed and watching while he took his capsules. He had a mild heart condition and the tablets were necessary for his health. He hated taking them though, and she had got into the habit of waiting till he did just in case he got it into that stubborn head of his to dispose of them after she had left the room.

'Yes what? Yes what? Don't just sit there and say yes!'

'You're not doing yourself any good with all this ranting and raving,' she said soothingly, removing the glass from him and handing him a mug of cocoa, which he stared at in loathing.

'Take that away from me,' he muttered ferociously. 'Bring me a proper drink. A gin and tonic! A whisky! Some brandy!'

'He may not even come,' she said, ignoring that request. 'Did he tell you when he'd be arriving?'

'Not in so many words. Knew I'd make sure the house was locked and bolted, probably.'

'Then if he hasn't told you definitely when he's coming, he probably won't turn up. Why is he planning on visiting after all this time, anyway?'

The old man shrugged and took the mug from her. 'Didn't say. Just said some rubbish about wanting to discuss a few things with me. What's there to discuss after all this time? Twelve years to be precise? What's there to discuss?'

Corinna gave that some thought and frowned. 'Who knows? Anyway, don't worry so much about it. Even if he does come, I'm sure you'll find that he's nothing like you remember. People change, after all. Life mellows them.'

'Stop philosophising. I hate it when people philosophise.'

She laughed and patted his hand affectionately. 'Go to sleep and wake up in a better temper.'

'You're going red from that sun.'

She laughed again and said drily from the door, 'Goodnight. Sweet dreams and don't forget the blood-pressure.'

As soon as she was in the downstairs drawing-room, she closed her eyes and settled comfortably in one of the chairs with her book.

This, like much else, had become a pleasant habit. Her girlfriends, whom she saw regularly at weekends, invariably asked her how she could stifle herself in the Surrey countryside when she had spent years working and living in London. They couldn't understand how peaceful it was at Deanbridge House, for all Benjamin Silver and his tempers. It suited her. She loved waking up to an absence of traffic, she loved the clean air, and she saw a great deal of London anyway, when she visited her friends. Most of them worked in busy London teaching hospitals and she constantly saw first-hand what she had left behind. True, there wasn't the constant rush of adrenalin as casualty cases were brought in day and night, needing urgent treatment, and maybe one day she would really miss all that and long to return to it, but right now this was just what she needed.

She had originally decided to do private nursing because she had become over-exhausted in her work, and for emotional reasons she needed to get out of London as well.

She stared down at the pages of her book but she wasn't seeing the fine black print. She was seeing Michael's face. Dear, sweet Michael to whom marriage had seemed almost inevitable. They had known each other from children and it had become accepted, over the years, that they were meant for each other. It had been a tacit understanding and it was only last year, at the age of twenty-two, when she had looked at him, with his good-natured smile, his undemanding amiability that she'd realised, quite suddenly, that she couldn't possibly marry him, however much a part of her craved that placid, undemanding security that he could offer.

She tried not to remember how upset he had been. It had not been an easy time. Her mother had been aggrieved. 'Darling,' she had said in that vaguely theatrical voice of hers, 'but you're so well *suited*.' Both so dull, Corinna had read behind the words. Her mother had a knack of insinuating an insult. Corinna had become accustomed to that, but at the time it had still hurt. She had grown up in the shadow of her mother's tempestuous, flamboyant personality. It had had the effect of making her overly cautious, mature beyond her years, practical, down-to-earth, and a part of her knew that that was just how her mother liked it. That way, her daughter could never be a threat to her.

Beyond coping with her mother's disappointment, though, she had had to cope with herself, with her own gut-wrenching suspicions that she was not built for love if she could not bring herself to love a man who was as kind and caring as Michael had been. Was something wrong with her? she had wondered.

She snapped shut the book and began prowling round the room, her eyes skimming over the tasteful drawing-room with its eighteenth-century wood panelling, its ivory, floor-length silk curtains, its marble mantelpiece. Very soothing colours. The furniture was fairly worn, but the warm, mellowed upholstery gave the room a pleasant glow, as did the small tables, dotted around the room, which were sprinkled with books of all kinds. It was one of Edna's bugbears that she liked neatness while

Benjamin insisted on leaving a trail of books behind him wherever he went.

'My eyes,' he was fond of telling her, 'are about the only useful things I have left. I might as well use them.'

In fact, her own position in the household, which was technically that of private nurse, was really more of a secretary-companion. Benjamin's health was poor, but not so poor that he really required any real nursing treatment, apart from ensuring that he took his tablets as prescribed and his blood-pressure was kept down. What he really wanted was someone who would take him for walks, talk to him, and help him with a historical piece of writing which he was doing on the house. With anyone else, Corinna acknowledged, it might have become boring, but Benjamin was too demanding and too intelligent for that ever to have been a problem.

Her thoughts turned to his son. Antonio Silver was the invisible presence that still filled Deanbridge House after all these years, although Benjamin would have been outraged if she had ever suggested as much. He liked to think that his son was little more than an aggravating memory, but it had been clear to Corinna from the very start that the old man ranted with the rage of a wounded bear.

Sometimes she thought that Antonio Silver couldn't possibly be as black as Benjamin portrayed him, but other times she felt an odd, protective anger against this unknown man who still had the power to hurt his own father. What kind of son was it who could cut the strings and leave without a backward glance?

In a strange way she could empathise with Benjamin. She, too, had been the victim of desertion. She only had dim memories of her father. He had left, after all, when she was still a child, left without a backward glance. For years she had wondered whether it was something she had said, something she had done. Maybe she had disappointed him. He had been so dramatic, so much larger than life, just like her mother, two people born to thrust daggers into each other until the effort of removing them had become too great—she had never been like that, passionate and extrovert. Had her own timid nature driven him away? Later, she knew that she had been a fool to have imagined any such thing, but a child's dark worries lingered far beyond the limits of sensible reason. She couldn't comprehend anyone who could relinquish their family ties the way Benjamin Silver's son had done. She knew from the occasional remark tossed in by Benjamin that he had divorced his wife somewhere along the way, and Antonio had left England to live with his mother in her native Italy, but would that have caused such a deep rift?

For the first time, she felt a deep, burning curiosity about this mysterious son. Previously, she had listened to Benjamin when he got on his soap box with her mind somewhere else, but now she wondered what his son really was like.

She was startled to discover when she next glanced at her watch that it had gone eleven, and she got up hurriedly, snapping shut her book and wondering whether she would ever finish it.

Early evenings were a luxury which she thoroughly enjoyed, after having spent years working crazy shifts at the hospital. Towards the end, she could remember being half dead on her feet, battling on in the wards despite an attack of flu which had kept her bed-ridden for a week and then tenaciously clung on, preying on her exhaustion. When, one morning, she had found herself physically incapable of getting out of bed, and no longer really caring whether she did or not, she realised that it was time for a much-needed break.

At this hour the house was totally silent. Edna and her husband, who was responsible for the gardens, were the only two people who lived in. The remainder of the staff were employed locally and they were invariably gone by eight-thirty, some much earlier.

She was walking past the front door when there was an almighty bang on it, followed by another.

Corinna wasn't a coward but she remained where she was, uncertainly wondering whether she should fetch Edna's husband Tom or else open the door herself. It was damned late for callers, or at least for those interested in socialising with Benjamin, but then burglars would hardly bang on the front door and expect entry. Or would they? She stood there, biting her lips in frustrated indecision, and only walked across to the door when the third heavy bang threatened to raise the household.

She carefully pulled open the door and then tried to shut it as her eyes took in the man standing outside, tall, powerful and with an aura of menace surrounding him.

It was a useless attempt, though. He pushed against it and her strength was no match for his. She fell back, and it was only when he was inside the hall that she realised that she had been holding her breath with fear.

Seeing him at close quarters and in the full glare of the overhead light did nothing to dispel the sensation of threat. She was a tall girl but he towered over her and the lean, hard build of his body spoke of a latent power. Her immediate impression was that this was not a man who took kindly to being crossed, which brought her back to the disturbing question: what if he was a burglar?

She folded her arms to stop herself from shivering and looked at him, her pupils dilated with fear.

'If you've come here to steal, then I'm afraid you've chosen the wrong house,' she said with as much authority as she could muster. 'There are two fierce dogs. I only have to whistle.'

She found that she couldn't take her eyes away from his face. It was such a striking face. A strong, sharp nose, above which black brows met in a fierce frown. Angular features which held the potential for cruelty, but a mouth that was strangely sensual and grey eyes which were now fixed on her with a tight, hostile expression.

He was dressed in black. Black trousers and a black jumper. Maybe, she thought, he might be less intimidating in a pair of shorts and a Hawaiian shirt.

'Really?' he said in a deep, ironic voice and with the very slightest trace of an accent. 'I've already had the pleasure of meeting your two fierce dogs. They escorted me to the front door.'

'Who are you?' She already knew, of course. Initially his sheer physical impact had done something to her brain, made it shut down, but the minute he spoke, she realised that he was Antonio Silver.

'I'm Benjamin Silver's son,' he said coolly, his hands thrust into his pockets, his eyes raking over her and then moving away to glance around him at his surroundings. He looked at her again and she had that same rattled, agitated feeling. 'But you know that, don't you? I can see it from the expression on your face. I take it my father received my letter.'

'You're not wanted here,' Corinna burst out and then was immediately horrified by what she had said.

His eyes narrowed on her and she felt herself go scarlet at the scrutiny.

'You must be Corinna Steadman,' he said with no attempt at politeness, 'my father's keeper.'

Something about his voice made her look at him warily. She felt like someone who was treading very carefully on a minefield and it wasn't a very pleasant sensation.

'I work for him, yes,' she said in a thin voice, 'I'm his private nurse.'

'That's not what I said.' He moved towards the front door and then turned to her. 'I'm going to fetch my case from the car,' he said with a cold smile that didn't contain the remotest hint of humour. 'Don't even think of slamming that door shut behind me.'

Corinna didn't say anything. She was still in a state of semi-shock, brought on, she decided, by the fact that he had appeared like a ghostly materialisation on the doorstep at the very moment she had been wondering about him. In a very short while the shock would wear off and she would be able to respond to him in a more controlled manner. In her profession, self-control was instilled as part of the training process and it wouldn't let her down.

He returned from the car with a tan leather holdall which he dumped on the ground, and she eyed it with resentment.

'I'm not about to carry that upstairs for you, like a porter,' she informed him, and was subjected to another of those freezing, ironic observations.

'I don't recall having asked. Or maybe you fancy yourself as a mind reader, as well as keeper of the house.'

'I don't fancy myself as anything of the sort!' she spluttered angrily, but he had turned away and was walking in the direction from which she had just come, towards the drawing-room, looking around him on the way.

She followed him, half running to keep up, with her arms folded across her chest.

'You can't just waltz in here——' she began, and he spun around to face her.

'And why not?' he asked coldly.

'Because,' she said nervously, 'because it's late and you should really come back tomorrow if you want to see your father. He's normally up and about by nine-thirty. I'll tell him you called.'

'You mean you'll warn him.' His lips stretched into an icy mimicry of a smile. 'No, thanks.'

He had very long legs. He stretched them out in front of him and crossed them at the ankles, clasping his hands behind his head.

'I feel as though I've never been away from here,' he said to himself, flicking those sharp grey eyes around and taking in everything. There was nothing, she decided uncomfortably, that this man missed. 'Nothing's changed at all; even those two pictures are in precisely the same place.'

'Nothing has to change!' Corinna said, hovering by the door.

She could tell immediately that he had temporarily forgotten about her presence and she wished that she had not reminded him of it because she was once again subjected to the brunt of that disturbing, hostile stare. He eyed her shortly and then commanded her to sit down. With some surprise, she found herself obeying, tentatively perching on the chair furthest away from him, a fact which didn't escape him from the look on his face.

'I'm glad I arrived when I did,' he surprised her by saying. 'No one about. No one but you.' There was something a little forbidding about the way he said that, and she shivered. 'It gives us the opportunity to chat.'

This man was arrogant, menacing and far too good-looking. Just the sort of man, she thought uneasily, that she had spent a lifetime conscientiously avoiding. Her father had been arrogant, good-looking, a magnet for other women. Over the years she had managed to submerge her feelings about her childhood into some safe, dark corner where she had firmly closed the door and, she had thought, thrown away the key. Now, though, memories rose up from those secret depths, memories of her father accusing her mother of having affairs, wild arguments in which they made no attempt to lower their voices, her mother shouting that what could he expect when he was fooling around behind her back as well? Antonio Silver, her inner voice told her, was a dangerous man.

'You're very protective about my father, aren't you?' His voice brought her hurtling back into the present.

'Yes, I am. I happen to be very fond of him.'

'So I gathered.'

She gave him a guarded, bewildered look and received another of those humourless smiles.

'I take it you're wondering what my source of information is?' he asked, and she didn't answer. She was getting more nervous by the minute. Where was her training when she needed it? she wondered crossly. She had spent years masking her expression with her patients, careful never to reveal too much, and with the doctors when their opinions had not coincided with her own, always cautious, always careful, and now here she was, red-faced and ill at ease.

'Angus McBride,' he said shortly, as if that should have explained everything, and she continued to look at him in uneasy bewilderment.

'Angus McBride told you...what?' Angus McBride was one of Benjamin's oldest friends. A lawyer who practised in the Midlands, he called in to visit whenever he was down south, which wasn't all that often. Corinna had liked him on sight. He was a small, thin man with a cheerful, shrewd face who didn't lack the courage to chide his friend for, as he put it, wasting his intellect away in the confines of Deanbridge House.

'Wrote and told me about you.'

'I had no idea that you kept in touch with anyone connected with your father.'

'And what other sweeping observations have you got on me?' he asked, staring at her from under his lashes.

'It wasn't a sweeping observation,' Corinna defended. 'It's just that from the way your father spoke...'

His grey eyes narrowed to slits and another wave of colour flooded over her. She would have to get her house in order, she thought, if she weren't to find herself completely obliterated by this man.

'So my father and you have been having lengthy discussions about me. Cosy.'

'That's not what I meant!' She stood up, agitated. 'You're putting words into my mouth! Your father and I haven't discussed you! I mean, your father talks about you now and again, but I don't respond. It's none of my business what goes on between the two of you! But I can't believe that Angus would write to you and tell tales.'

'Whoever mentioned telling tales? He's the family lawyer and we've kept in touch over the years. He wrote to me a few months ago telling me about you, or at any rate about a nurse who had started working for my father. Since then your name has cropped up several times, in the most glowing of terms, might I add.'

'I don't see what you're getting at.'

'Don't you? You don't strike me as a stupid girl. Well, to ease you out of your bewilderment, let me just put it like this. My father is a very wealthy man. This house alone is worth a small fortune and he has other properties as well, quite a few of them dotted throughout London and all carrying very respectable price tags on them.'

Corinna didn't let him finish. She stormed towards him, her hands on her hips and looked down at that arrogant, dark head furiously.

'So I'm after your father's money, is that it?' She gave him a scathing look. 'I would be insulted by that accusation if it came from anyone else but you! As far as I'm concerned, you're not exactly qualified to troop along here and accuse me of *anything*, considering you haven't seen fit to set foot in this house for God knows how many years! You're hardly the loving son, are you?'

She should have guessed that he wouldn't take too kindly to insults. He had the easygoing friendliness of a python, after all, and his hand snapped out to hold her by the wrist while he stared at her disdainfully.

'Spare me your observations on my character,' he said through gritted teeth.

'Why should I?' Corinna asked with equal hostility. 'I haven't noticed you sparing me *your* observations on *my* character!'

He released her abruptly and she massaged her wrist, trying to get the blood circulation going again.

'Why should I?' he asked too, standing up and prowling round the room, his hands stuffed into his pockets. Corinna followed his movements reluctantly. He moved with the easy grace of someone who was well aware of the physical impact of his presence. He was a tall man, well over six feet, and he carried his height with a confidence that sent a shiver of alarm running through her. She couldn't remember ever following Michael's movements with this avidity and she tore her eyes away with a stern reminder to herself that not only was this man highly objectionable, the stuff of nightmares in fact, but he was also insulting and offensive. And she had been stupid enough to give him the benefit of the doubt by imagining that his father had exaggerated his flaws. If anything he had understated them.

He had stopped in front of the marble mantelpiece and he turned to look at her from across the room. It took enormous effort to steel herself against the scrutiny. It was like being cross-examined, she thought, and, worse, it made her feel guilty, as though she had something to hide, when in fact she didn't.

'I'm not the intruder,' he said. 'My last name is Silver.'

'What a charming way with introductions you have,' Corinna threw at him. 'Are you usually such a sociable character?'

'When it comes to women like you, I don't see the necessity for polite exchanges. Bluntness is the only tool you types understand.'

'Women like me? Types?' she all but shouted. No one had ever made her so angry in her life before. She had always been a very controlled person, not given to displays of temper. In fact, she found displays of temper alarming and often unnecessary, uneasy reminders of her childhood spent on her parents' battleground. So it amazed her that this perfect stranger had managed to antagonise her to the point where she felt very much inclined to reach for the nearest heavy object and sling it at him. She took a few steadying breaths and said carefully, 'I don't have to stand for this. It's hardly my fault if you swan in here, in the middle of the night, acting as though you've caught me trying to steal the family silver. Anyway, as far as I'm concerned, you're the intruder. You haven't contacted your father in years, not even so much as a Christmas card, and——'

'You seem to have mastered the fine art of jumping to conclusions,' he threw at her forcefully.

'Your father told me——'

'I'm sick of hearing what my father told you! Do you actually have any time to do the work you're presumably paid for in between all these riveting conversations you appear to have with him?'

Corinna stared at him furiously, bereft of speech. It wasn't fair, she thought, Antonio Silver should be middle-aged, he should be overweight and dull. She would have been able to cope with overweight and dull.

'It's late,' she said tightly. 'I'm going to bed.' She turned on her heel but she hadn't made it to the door when he was in front of her, barring her exit. She hadn't even heard him move. Businessman? she thought sourly. This man was a businessman? Terrorist more likely.

'You're not going anywhere until I'm through with you.'

'Until you're through with me?' she asked, glaring up at him. Her long hair was in its habitual plait. It had swung over her shoulder and lay on her breast like a silver rope. 'Until you're through with me? Just who do you think you are?'

'Someone you should be afraid of, someone who isn't about to be taken in by those big eyes and reassuring bedside manner which, I suspect, you've been laying on thick ever since you set foot into this house! You've already shown me the roar behind that carefully nurtured mousy façade. God knows, I'm surprised you don't play havoc with his blood-pressure.'

Their eyes clashed and she was the first to look away. Very hurriedly. Up this close she could almost breathe in his masculinity. It seemed to go straight to her head like incense, making her feel giddy and unstable on her feet.

'Not as much as you will,' she muttered, and he leaned towards her, as if trying to ascertain what she had said. She found herself tempted to step backwards.

'What was that?'

'I said that I'd better show you to your room if you intend to spend the night here.'

'Now whatever gave you the idea that I intended spending the night here?'

'Your bag?' she said in the tone of someone talking to a complete idiot, and she was pleased to find that there wasn't a hint of a tremor in her voice, even though her hands were trembling. 'The fact that it's gone midnight and you'd be hard pressed to find anywhere else to stay?'

He didn't appear in the least put out by her tone, though.

'Oh, you're on the wrong tack,' he said with a cool smile, and she brightened.

'You mean you won't be staying here?' That would please Benjamin no end, she thought, because if his son was going to be under the same roof, then who knew what sort of problems would arise? He would never stand for it, she knew. He would collapse on the spot, or else have Edna throw him out on his ear. She eyed Antonio sceptically. No, perhaps not. Even ferocious Edna had her limits.

'Oh, yes,' he said casually, killing her short-lived optimism. 'But not for one night. I'm here for an indefinite length of time.'

'An indefinite length of time?' she repeated, dismayed, and he smiled slowly at her discomfiture.

'I can see you find the prospect appealing.'

Appealing? Corinna thought faintly. Was the prospect of death by slow torture appealing? Was a charging bull appealing?

'But you haven't brought enough luggage,' she said faintly.

'There are two cases in the car,' he said, and she could see that he was deriving cruel amusement at her expense. 'And before you launch into another speech on the definition of your duties, I don't expect you to carry them up to the bedroom for me. We wouldn't want you to sully your fair hands with such a menial task, would we?'

'But why?' she asked, ignoring the sneer with effort. 'Why have you suddenly decided to come to England and moreover stay under the same roof as your father?'

'Two reasons, my dear Miss Steadman. The first is because one of my companies is opening a subsidiary over here, not terribly far away from Deanbridge House, in fact, in Guildford.'

'And the second?'

'The second,' he said softly, there was open threat in his voice, 'is so that I can keep an eye on you. We wouldn't want you to start getting ideas beyond your station, now, would we?'

# CHAPTER TWO

CORINNA had no idea how she managed to get to sleep.
By the time her head had hit the pillow, she had been
positively shaking with anger. She couldn't remember
ever having been so riled by anyone in her life before.
Her wonderful self-control, which she was convinced
would stand her in good stead despite having deserted
her initially, remained conspicuous by its absence, and
she could have screamed in frustration as she lay down
under the quilt and tried to court sleep. It was a long
time coming, though. Her head was too full of images
of Antonio Silver.

The following morning she got up and all those images
which had seared her mind the previous night rushed
back to her in sickening detail.

It was not a great way to start the day. For the past
few months, after she had become accustomed to living
in Deanbridge House, she had awakened slowly and
contentedly, never failing to be charmed by the mint-
green luxury of the bedroom with its heavy drapes cas-
cading to the floor, the exquisite pieces of furniture, the
cool softness of the beige-coloured carpet underfoot.

This morning she found herself not giving a moment's
thought to her surroundings and she made herself slow
down. This man, she decided, was not going to get under
her skin again. He had managed that the night before
because he had caught her unawares, when she was tired
and vulnerable and unable to defend herself, but today
he would find himself facing an altogether different
cup of tea.

She took her time dressing, brushing her long hair carefully and knotting it behind her head in a chignon, by far the most practical hairstyle for her. She never wore a nurse's uniform, having been informed by Benjamin on day one that he wouldn't tolerate her clumping around in heavy shoes and a starchy white frock, but she always made sure that she dressed smartly. Never trousers and never shorts, despite the fact that it was quite hot at the moment. She had a good supply of sober, unfussy skirts and blouses and she extracted an oatmeal skirt from the wardrobe and a crisp, beige short-sleeved shirt, then looked at her reflection in the mirror.

Nothing, she acknowledged realistically, to write home about. She supposed she wasn't bad-looking in an average sort of way, but for the first time since she had started working for Benjamin she realised that her wardrobe didn't do a great deal for her. With her fair complexion she needed to wear things that were dramatic, that put colour in her cheeks, instead of a selection of background outfits that made her appear drained.

How was it that she was only now noticing this trait? Mousy. That was what he had called her. Had she cultivated this drabness as a subconscious reaction to her mother? It seemed likely, and she felt an unexpected anger that circumstances could mould a person so completely. Her parents' divorce had been a background tune playing in the back of her mind for as long as she could remember. Too long.

On the spur of the moment she added a touch of blusher to her cheeks and then frowned impatiently at herself.

Would Benjamin have been notified of Antonio's presence? she wondered, as she walked briskly down the corridor towards his bedroom. She had deliberately taken

her time this morning because she didn't want to appear
over-keen to find out, but she was dying of curiosity.

As soon as she entered the bedroom she was aware
that he had already heard the bad news. The curtains
had not been drawn back, and that was usually the first
thing he did in the morning, and the room was in
darkness. He was lying on the bed and she approached
him tentatively.

'Good morning, Benjamin,' she said brightly, moving
to pull the curtains, and he said in a woebegone voice,

'Why bother? I won't be getting out of bed this
morning.'

She ignored that and drew back the curtains, letting
in a flood of early morning sunshine.

'Come along,' she said with a beaming smile, and he
glared at her.

'And you can stop being chirpy. That—that *son of
mine* has dared to cross the threshold of this house!' The
woebegone expression was beginning to lift and some of
his ranting energies were back in place.

'I know,' Corinna said quietly, tidying up the room,
even though one of the girls would later be coming in
to clean.

'You know!' he roared. 'You know and you didn't
even tell me?'

'He arrived very late last night,' she said, trying not
to let her memory of that disastrous encounter show on
her face. 'Just as I was about to retire for the evening,
in fact.'

'Typical!' Benjamin roared with some of his usual fire.
'Typical! Never spares so much as a passing thought to
anyone else! Typical!'

'And how do you find out about his arrival?' She
busied herself stacking his books into a neat pile on the
long, low table by the window.

'Edna. Trooping up here at the crack of dawn to break the happy news! Damned woman thought that I'd be delighted, even though I've spent years making it perfectly clear how I felt about him! What a fool! Ruined my day, of course. I couldn't touch a mouthful of my breakfast, and I'm certainly not coming downstairs. Not until he's well and truly out of the place!'

He glared at her aggressively and she tried to give him a soothing, professional smile.

'He doesn't seem to be in much of a hurry to leave,' she said, choosing her words carefully, and he shot her a baleful look.

'He'll be in a hurry,' Benjamin said, flapping his arms about and looking quite comical. 'Oh, he'll be in a hurry when I set the dogs—the—Edna—the police on him!'

Personally Corinna didn't think that the police would feel much inclined to storm the place and capture Antonio Silver by force simply because his father didn't want him around, but she refrained from saying anything.

'You can't stay in bed all day,' she pointed out reasonably. 'You'll be bored stiff in under an hour. Besides, I may take you for walks in your wheelchair, but you know that you need to exercise your limbs by walking around the house. You know what the doctor said——'

'I refuse to budge. I don't care what you or that quack of a doctor says.'

'Dr Harman isn't a quack, in fact, he's noted——'

'Noted, boted,' Benjamin cut in with rising irritation. 'I'm not budging. Though why I should be a prisoner in my own home I fail to understand. This is my home, dammit! How dare he walk in here and shut me up in my bedroom? You'll have to get him out!'

'What, me?' She stopped what she was doing and then looked wryly at him as he gave her a sly smile.

'So, I see he's got to you, has he? What did you think of him, then?'

'If you must know,' she said calmly, 'I thought he was overbearing, arrogant and unpleasant.'

'But good-looking, eh? He used to be damned fine-looking when I last saw him. What does he look like now?' He glanced down at his gnarled fingers and then clasped them on his lap, continuing to peer at them with overdone fascination.

'Passable,' Corinna said. She extracted some clothes from his wardrobe and laid them out on the bed. Grey flannel trousers, a pale blue long-sleeved shirt because Benjamin had no time for short-sleeved shirts, whatever the weather, a pair of charcoal-grey socks.

She could feel her heart step up a beat as she remembered Antonio Silver's formidable physical impact. In the cold light of day he was probably no-where as overwhelming as he had appeared the night before, but she still couldn't prevent the tell-tale flush of colour on her cheeks.

Benjamin, though, wasn't looking at her. He was still peering at his hands.

'Well, I won't see him,' he said finally, 'so you might as well put those clothes right where you found them.'

'Now don't be silly,' she began, and he lay down on his side and pretended that she wasn't there. She wasn't at all perturbed by this reaction. Benjamin Silver could be childishly truculent at times. He had a fine, sharp mind that had been blunted by disuse. Too little mental stimulation filled him with an energy which his body did not allow him to exhaust and his way of coping was to try and rule the roost around him. Angus McBride was right, he needed more than the walls of Deanbridge House to fill his days.

'You'll have to face him some time,' she said bluntly. 'He doesn't look like the type who's going to disappear just because you want him to. I know that it's your house, but honestly, what can you do? You'll just have to face him.'

'Did he say why he'd come?' he asked in a muffled voice, and she stiffened, recalling the conversation with a feeling of remembered unpleasantness.

'That's something you'll have to discuss with him,' she said, looking down, and he rolled over to face her.

'My curiosity isn't that great,' he informed her loftily and she shrugged. She was beginning to feel like piggy in the middle and it was a feeling for which she had no taste. Why did Antonio Silver have to appear on the scene? Things were going so smoothly in her life. For the first time in ages, she felt truly relaxed, having quit her job and left Michael, two aspects of her life which she only realised in retrospect had been pulling her down. Why had he come along and spoilt everything with his accusations and his sophisticated mockery?

She opened her mouth to inform him that there was no way that she was going to play intermediary, but before she could speak he was waving his hand in a gesture of dismissal.

'Shoo!' he said. 'Have the day off. Just so long as you keep that so-called son of mine out of my hair!'

With a cross sigh of defeat, she left the room, quietly shutting the door behind her and made her way downstairs to the kitchen.

There was a parlour which had been specifically designed to be used as a breakfast-room, but neither she nor Benjamin ever used it in that capacity. The kitchen was a much warmer place. It was Edna's pride and joy and in the entire house it was the one room to which no concessions to glamour had been made. Only the cooking utensils were the best that money could buy, because Edna prided herself on her cooking. She never allowed any of the girls to help her, cultivated her own personal herb garden, and produced simple but lovely fare. She was a great fan of the roast meal, and detested things with too much cream or alcohol as being travesties of good cooking.

'Sure road to indigestion,' she was fond of saying. Benjamin, of course, was wont to inform her that she was clearly behind the times, but he too preferred simple cooking, so the arrangement suited him perfectly.

Corinna walked into the kitchen wearing a frown of concentration and immediately stopped dead in her tracks. She had all but convinced herself that Antonio Silver was only an ordinary human being, a mere mortal with no more than a bit of an acid temperament, but seeing him now, sitting at the kitchen table with a cup of black coffee in front of him, casually dressed in a beige shirt which had been rolled to the elbows to expose his strong forearms, she felt a sudden urge to turn tail and flee. He was every bit as commanding as her very worst memories. In the light of day, she could see that every bone in his face was stamped with hard, self-assured assertiveness. He was darker than she had thought, his skin bearing the hallmark of a life in a kinder climate, which made his silver-grey eyes appear more startling because of the contrast.

He watched her as she poured herself a cup of coffee, and, when she had sat down, he finally said politely, 'Good morning.'

'Good morning,' Corinna returned awkwardly, shifting her gaze away from his probing stare. 'Did you sleep well?' she asked politely, and he raised his eyebrows as if ironically amused by the lack of sincerity in her question. The open hostility was no longer quite as apparent as it had been the night before, but it was still there, of that she had no doubt, simmering away under the surface, temporarily replaced by an equally disconcerting iciness. If only that could distract her from his intense physical appeal, but she was alarmed to find that her body was reacting to his blatant masculinity with edgy awareness.

'I've had better nights,' he returned, sipping some coffee and looking at her over the brim of the cup. 'I trust you've seen my father and informed him of my presence?'

'He already knew before I saw him this morning. Edna told him.'

'And?'

'And what?' She fixed him with a blank, innocent stare. She would have preferred not to be sitting here, not to be struggling with her treacherous, racing nerves, but, since she was, she wasn't about to indulge in open warfare. If this was a cold war, then she would play the rules of that game.

'And what was his reaction?'

Corinna gave it some thought. Appear calm and collected, she thought, and you'll feel calm and collected. 'He wasn't a hundred per cent impressed,' she told him calmly. There was fresh bread on the table. She took a slice and buttered it, making sure not to look at him. Passable, she realised, was not an adequate description of Antonio Silver. He had the build of an athlete, his body hard and finely tuned, and a face which would make most women stop dead in their tracks, and no doubt he was very much aware of that. Conceited, she decided at once. The man was probably brimming over with conceit, as well as being thoroughly dislikeable, and conceit was hardly one of the world's most admirable characteristics, was it?

She could feel those silver-grey eyes on her and she looked up with a polite, detached expression.

'Not a hundred per cent impressed,' he drawled lazily, sitting back in the chair to give her the full benefit of his attention. 'I had forgotten that you British were the masters of understatement.'

'We British? Aren't you forgetting that you're at least half British? Surely not; you made such a point of reminding me of that fact last night.'

There was a brief silence, then he unexpectedly smiled, and that smile filled his face with such devastatingly sexy charm that she felt her cheeks go pink in sudden confusion. She almost found herself preferring the angry insults to this.

'Where's Edna?' she asked quickly, not caring to dwell on the impact he was making on her.

'Gone to the village. My father may be unimpressed with my arrival, but Edna thinks it's the return of the prodigal son. She's gone to stock up on all my favourite foods. God knows how she remembered them. She must have the memory of an elephant.'

So, she thought sourly, the formidable Edna has turned pussycat. He probably had that reaction from every woman he came into contact with.

'And where's my father?' he asked, lowering his eyes in almost precisely the same manner that Benjamin had a short while ago.

'In his bedroom.'

'Hiding?'

It was so near the mark that she was taken aback. 'Trying to get over the shock of realising that you're here,' she said tartly. 'I don't think he wants to see you, at least not at the moment.' Maybe you could try again

in a few years' time, she thought, when I'm well and
truly out of here.

'Well, he's going to see me whether he likes it or not,'
Antonio said coolly, 'and without you playing the little
mediator. No doubt running between the two of us would
give you no end of pleasure, but I intend to see him and
that's that.'

'I can't think of anything worse than running between
the two of you,' Corinna said tightly, already beginning
to feel rattled. 'He's your father, you sort your troubles
out yourself.'

'And I won't have you trying to influence him either.'

She slammed her cup down on the table and looked
at him angrily. 'I have no intention of trying to influence
your father!' she informed him.

'So you haven't told him what we discussed last night?'

'No,' she said in a more controlled voice, 'I haven't
told him what *you* discussed last night. *I* don't recall
having discussed anything with you.'

'And you haven't run to him with any derogatory de-
scriptions of me?'

Corinna opened her mouth and closed it.

'Trying to find an appropriate lie to that one?' he asked
her, looking at her coldly.

'He asked me what my impression was of you, and I
told him the truth.'

'Which was . . . ?'

'That you struck me as being arrogant and
objectionable.'

She expected him to hit the roof with that one, but
he didn't, and she shifted uneasily in the chair.

'I can't think of too many women who have called me
that before,' he said softly, staring at her, and she thought
to herself, No, I don't suppose you have, I suppose
they've all been too busy trying to get you to give them

one of those lazy, charming smiles of yours. Well, not me, buster.

'No?' she asked politely. 'They must be very short-sighted, then.'

'Or maybe you're the one with the misguided judgement. You are, after all, in a minority. Of course, you could be an expert on men. Is that it?'

'I forgot one more adjective,' she said, ignoring his question, and he raised his eyebrows in a question. 'Egotistical.'

'Now might I be permitted to subject you to the same character assassination as you've just subjected me to?' he asked, and she reddened, not saying anything.

Her coffee had gone cold and she refilled her cup, not liking this turn in the conversation one bit. She didn't want to get involved in any word games with this man. In fact, she would have liked to be able to ignore his presence completely.

'Do I have a choice?' she asked. 'I gather you'll force your opinions on me whether I like them or not. You did last night.'

'Well,' he said, folding his arms and looking at her from under his thick, black lashes, 'you're a relatively plain little creature, but I wouldn't describe you as background material. No, quite fiery in fact, and with lots of that so-called honesty which some English people think is a virtue when in fact it's only a mark of rudeness.'

'A mark of rudeness . . . !' she spluttered, furious.

'That's right,' he agreed silkily. 'Have you cultivated that in an attempt to win my father over? I remember him as being brilliant and temperamental, a man who wouldn't be able to abide any coy simpering around him. Did you think that the quickest and surest way to win him over was to meet fire with fire?'

'I don't have to stay here and listen to this.' She stood up, trembling, and turned to go.

'Wait!'

'Don't order me about! You might get away with that where you come from and with the sort of women you mix with, but not me!'

They stared at each other and she felt a heated, unwelcome awareness of his masculinity. When he stood up, she had to force herself not to move, to remain where she was when every confused instinct was telling her to run. He walked across to her, not taking his eyes off her face, and she glared at him with resentment. Plain, was she? Scheming, was she? She wished that the ground would open and swallow him up. She would stand and watch him disappearing with a smile.

'The sort of women I mix with?'

'You heard me! From what you said they fall at your feet, but don't expect the same sort of reaction from me!'

He looked at her speculatively, as if digesting that remark, and she wished that she hadn't said anything. There was no reason why she had to defend herself to this man and it irked her that she was continually being forced into a position of self-defence.

'No?' he said, watching her mouth, then flicking his eyes along her body, then back to her face. 'The financial reward not tempting enough?' Her face darkened and he laughed with acid amusement. 'Or maybe the little mouse with the fiery temper prefers to scurry into a corner and observe life from the sidelines?'

He was deliberately antagonising her. It was obvious. But the desire to wipe that cool assessing sneer off his dark face was so strong that she had to clench her fists tightly to overcome it.

'Is there anything else you want or can I leave?'

'Which is my father's bedroom?'

She began telling him but he interrupted her and said, 'Take me there. I think the time for confrontation has arrived.'

She nodded and spun round, walking briskly into the hall, then up the staircase to the right wing of the house, tensely aware of his presence behind her. Was he nervous? she wondered. He didn't appear nervous. In fact, he gave the impression of someone who didn't have a nervous bone in his body, but he could just be a good actor. She tried to imagine him having butterflies in his stomach and failed.

They had reached Benjamin's bedroom and she knocked on the door, pushing it open and stepping in.

She wasn't looking at Antonio, so she didn't see his reaction, but Benjamin's face mirrored his shock. She had a strange feeling of being superfluous and made to move away, but Benjamin bellowed at her, 'Where do you think you're going? I told you that I didn't want to see him!'

Antonio's mouth hardened but he didn't say anything. He walked into the room, round to the side of the bed, and stood there looking down at his father, his face unreadable. It didn't look as though it had the makings of a touching emotional reunion and Corinna reluctantly entered the room as well, shutting the door behind her.

'You're not wanted here,' Benjamin said breathlessly, beckoning to her to come over, which she did, and then clasping her hand tightly, all of which she could see his son noting, jotting down, no doubt, in that computer mind of his to be recalled and used against her at a later date.

'My heart,' Benjamin said, 'my blood-pressure. I can't take this. The shock will kill me.' He lay back looking faint and Antonio shot her a doubtful look.

'I did write to tell you that I'd be coming,' he said, reverting his eyes to Benjamin who had his eyes closed and was breathing heavily.

'Perhaps you'd better leave,' Corinna interjected worriedly, reaching next to the bed for her bag which contained her instruments. If Benjamin's blood-pressure was up, then Antonio would have to leave whether he liked it or not.

He ignored her. 'Didn't you receive my letter?'

'I preferred to think that it had been a mistake.' He opened his blue eyes and peered at his son with defensive hostility on his face. Side by side, she could see the resemblance between them, which had not been so noticeable before. Their features weren't identical by any means, and Antonio, with his deeply bronzed skin, looked distinctly foreign, but there was a similarity of expression stamped on both their faces, the same strong, stubborn look in their eyes. Two forceful personalities, she thought, destined to clash.

'I never make mistakes,' Antonio said, glancing at her, and she returned his look with equanimity.

'Well, you made a mistake coming over here,' Benjamin said. 'You haven't set foot in this house for years and that's suited me just fine. As far as I am concerned, I haven't got a son.'

That brought a dark flush to Antonio's cheeks, but whether it stemmed from anger or discomfort, Corinna couldn't say.

'We both know the reasons that I left here in the first place,' he answered tautly. 'Not,' he continued harshly, 'that I want to have our dirty linen aired in front of your nurse.'

'Why not?' Benjamin threw at him, 'she's more a part of my life than you are.'

'A dangerous situation, wouldn't you say?' Antonio said grimly. 'She's a nurse, she's not indispensable.'

'Will the two of you stop talking as if I weren't here!' Corinna burst out. She faced Benjamin and said quietly, 'Your son's right, I shouldn't be here. The two of you should talk your differences out without a third party present.'

'I have nothing to talk out,' Benjamin said stubbornly. He looked at his son, one hand clenched. 'I didn't invite you here. I don't know why you've come and I don't want to know. Just seeing you is going to set my blood-pressure soaring.'

'It's fine,' Corinna said. She had taken it unobtrusively a short while ago and was surprised to find that it had been stable.

'For the moment,' Benjamin growled, 'but not if I have to be subjected to this sort of scene for much longer.'

Antonio gave an impatient click of his tongue. 'Look, I've been away a long time,' he muttered, glancing across to where Corinna was standing. 'I grant you that all this should have been cleared up a long time ago.'

His face was tight, and she could tell straight away that he was not a man who felt comfortable making concessions of any description.

'Should have been, but wasn't,' Benjamin said, refusing to bend. 'Now if you don't mind leaving, I feel very tired. Close the door behind you.'

Antonio shook his head and spun round on his heel, slamming the door behind him.

'Well?' Benjamin muttered to Corinna. 'Don't just stand there pretending that you have nothing to say. And for God's sake stop fussing around these damned bedclothes! What are you thinking? You might as well tell me instead of wearing that tight-lipped expression.'

Corinna hesitated, then said, 'You could have handled that a bit better.'

'A bit better? A bit better! So he's got to you, has he? That's the way the ground lies, is it?'

'Don't be foolish. Nobody's got to me. I just think that you could have accepted his apology.'

'Why?'

'Because it might have been the start of some kind of truce between you.'

'It's a truce I could do without.'

She shrugged and Benjamin's eyebrows met in a frown. 'He's not wanted and don't try and be saintly. Didn't it strike you that he doesn't approve of you? Dispensable, he called you, I believe.'

She lowered her eyes. 'It doesn't bother me.'

'Well, it bothers me. I don't want to hear what he's got to say, and if part of the reason that he's found his way here is because he's got to know about you and thinks you might have designs on my bank balance, then he's wasted his time.'

Corinna looked at him, startled. She had known that Benjamin was shrewd, but his astuteness amazed her.

'So I'm right, am I?'

'How did you guess?'

'I suppose that fool Angus has written to him about you,' he said, continuing when he saw her bewildered expression. 'He's been trying to get us together for years. Keeps in touch with Antonio, you see. Throws me titbits about his life every now and again to whet my appetite, no doubt, as if I'm interested.' He gave a shout of laughter. 'Well, I'm not about to forgive and forget as easily as that!'

'You're a stubborn old man,' she said with resigned affection. 'You know what they say about pride.'

'And you know what I say about you philosophising,' he retorted. 'Now could you go and fuss somewhere else?'

'You're not coming down?'

'Not at the moment.'

'And what about food?'

'Get that witch Edna to bring it to me. It's time she worked for her keep.' He closed his eyes, his way of dismissing her, and she let herself out of the room quietly.

As she looked up she saw Antonio waiting for her, lounging against the wall at the top of the stairs, and she did her best to walk past him, but he wasn't about to let her. He reached out and held her and for some reason which she could only put down to dislike, her body began doing strange things. Her skin tingled where his fingers were curled round her forearm and she found that she was breathing quickly, as if she had just run a marathon.

'I've been waiting for you,' he said grimly.

'Take your hand off me.'

That had the opposite effect of making him grip her tighter.

'I watched you,' he said, 'the way my father responds to you.'

'How interesting. Now do you mind?'

'I don't know how you've done it but you've managed to become a necessary part of his life. I won't let you take him for a ride.'

Her eyes flashed angrily as she contemplated that statement. 'You're not in a position to put your foot down on anything, *Mr Antonio Silver*. Not that there's anything to put your foot down about, anyway! And not that it's any of my business, but all this sudden rush

of concern for your father, how do I know that it's not
because you feel your inheritance being compromised?
Is that why you flew over here at a rate of knots the
minute you heard about me?'

His mouth thinned. 'You're right, it's none of your
business, but I'll set your little mind at rest anyway. I
don't need my father's estates. I have enough money of
my own to buy my own estates.'

'Oh.'

'Satisfied?' he sneered. 'Or would you like to see a
few of my bank balances?'

'You can't blame me for thinking...' she muttered,
and he jerked her towards him.

'Keep your thoughts to yourself in the future,' he said
through clenched teeth. 'You're a nurse, have you forgotten? You're not here to speculate on things that don't
concern you, you're here for my father's health, though
I'm surprised you haven't driven him into the grave with
that tongue of yours.'

That hurt. 'That's unfair,' she whispered, looking
down, and there was silence. 'Your father and I get along
well together.'

'Too well.'

'I resent your assumptions. If what you're aiming at
is to force me from this house, then you're wasting your
time. I like it here, I like your father, and that has nothing
to do with the size of his bank balance! Your cynicism
might help you in that concrete jungle you live in, but
it's out of place here!'

'Is it?' He gave that some thought, and she looked at
his downturned eyes, the dark sweep of his lashes, a little
uneasily.

'All right. We'll have it your way. Maybe I misjudged
you.' His voice was soft and smooth. 'I must admit that

when I came over here I didn't expect to find someone like you.'

The question was too tempting to resist. 'What did you expect to find?'

'Someone,' he drawled lazily, 'a bit sexier. A bit more—filled out, so to speak. And definitely a brunette. My father has only ever been attracted to dark-haired women, did you know that? That's a little titbit for your scrap-book, isn't it?'

There was something dangerously hypnotic about his deep voice and steel-grey eyes.

'How do you know that?' she asked calmly, blinking away the desire to be mesmerised.

'A confidence exchanged a long time ago. A passing remark that's stuck in my head over the years.'

So, the thought struck her, there must have been warmth there at one point. What had gone wrong? She would never ask either of them and she had a feeling that the information would never be forthcoming.

He was looking at her with intense concentration and she began to feel even more uncomfortable.

'What are your plans now?' she asked, trying to get the subject on to more neutral ground.

'You already know what my plans are. I have work to do here, apart from everything else.'

I hope it keeps you out of the house, she thought, viewing a succession of fraught encounters with something approaching panic.

'Fine,' she said, 'now could you let me go? You seem to enjoy taking the caveman approach with me, but I'd really prefer you to keep your hands to yourself.'

'If you say so.' He let go of her, then said before she could walk away, 'But first——' he reached behind her and unpinned her hair in one easy movement and it cascaded down to her waist, long, straight and like spun silk '—I've been intrigued to see whether you're as icy and untouchable-looking with your hair loose.'

Vivid colour flowed into her face. She could feel her heart beating like a drum inside her chest and for once she couldn't think of a thing to say. Without a word, she began walking away.

'Wouldn't like to know what I think?' she heard him ask from behind her, and there was amused laughter in his voice.

Damn him! Was his opinion of her so low that he felt he could do and say anything he pleased to her? The back of her neck was still prickling from where his fingers had brushed against it and, whether she admitted it or not, her blood was racing with a terrible, forbidden excitement.

# CHAPTER THREE

BENJAMIN didn't emerge from his room until the following morning, by which time he had harnessed some of his raging temper, at least as far as Corinna could make out. She laid out his clothes on his bed, and he emerged from his bedroom half an hour later with a few additions to what she had set out. A blue silk cravat and the comfortable loafers which he normally used around the house had been discarded in favour of a pair of tan shoes which looked far too smart for everyday use.

Corinna eyed him with some amusement and he scowled at her.

'Something the matter?' he barked, allowing her to take his arm as they walked down the staircase.

'You look very dapper,' she said seriously. 'Are you going somewhere?'

'Can't a man look halfway smart in his own house?' Benjamin barked, 'without being subjected to wisecracks?'

'I wasn't being funny!'

'Well, it sounded that way to me,' he muttered grumpily, and she grinned. 'Where is he, anyway?'

'Oh, have you dressed to impress?'

'I have not!' he denied with a little too much vigour. 'Why would I do that? I don't even want him under my roof!'

'Well, I don't know where he is.' They had reached the kitchen and Corinna began laying out his breakfast. Kippers, toast, coffee, juice, while Benjamin took his place at the table and eyed her speculatively.

'You seem to have improved your image a bit as well,' he commented slyly, 'now that we're on the subject.'

Corinna didn't look at him but she felt her face redden. All right, so she had decided to wear a little make-up and a deep pink blouse with a matching skirt instead of the usual invisible colours she favoured, but that didn't mean anything at all. It certainly didn't mean that she was trying to create any sort of impression on Antonio Silver, because she wasn't. She hadn't seen him at all since his arrogant gesture in releasing her hair, just for fun, and in the interim she had decided that she really loathed the man. She didn't like his massive self-confidence bordering on downright arrogance, she didn't like his too striking good looks, she didn't like his easy, sexual charm lurking just below the surface, and most of all she didn't like the way he always managed to get under her skin and do strange things to her composure. She had always been a very composed girl and she meant to stay that way. Men like that frightened her. They were too powerful, too clever, too self-assured. She had always longed for the non-threatening. Hadn't she?

'Well?' Benjamin prodded in his usual forthright manner, which she was beginning to see wasn't all that different from his son's. 'So what's behind the charming pink outfit which, might I say, is far and away the nicest thing I've seen you in since you were here?'

'Nothing,' Corinna remarked, pouring herself a mug of coffee and sitting down. 'And if you think that there is, then your imagination's running away with you.'

'A bit like yours was a minute ago,' he said mildly, crunching into his toast, and she looked at him with resigned exasperation.

'Well, now that we've sorted that one out,' she said after a while, 'what are we going to do today? Shall we take the usual walk and then spend some time on your writing, or would you like to do something different? We could go to the local library. You've been talking about needing some books which you haven't got in your library.'

'Yes, why don't you?' The deep, familiar voice threw them both into startled confusion and Corinna looked up, her blue eyes clashing with Antonio's.

The first thought that raced through her brain was that he seemed to look more damned attractive every time she saw him. He was clearly on his way out somewhere, because he was wearing a suit, a deep grey, double-breasted one that made him seem more aggressively good-looking if that was possible.

Hard on the heels of this thought came another, namely that good-looking men weren't to be trusted, a piece of advice which her mother had bitterly given her years ago, and which had stuck in her head like a refrain from a well-loved song.

Benjamin had stopped eating and was staring at his son, and she could see that all the old antagonism was back, not that that deterred Antonio. He sat down at the head of the table and watched them both with a shuttered expression.

'It would do you good to get out,' he said conversationally, and Benjamin erupted.

'And who do you think you are dispensing advice to *me*?' he roared. 'Not only do you see fit to swan into my house, *against my wishes*, but now you're telling me how to run my life! What next? Telling me what books I should read, perhaps? Or what clothes I should be wearing?'

Antonio's lips had thinned and Corinna looked at him with consternation.

'I'm here now,' he said, in what she suspected was a huge attempt to remain reasonable, 'so can't we stop jumping down each other's throats and start acting like two adults?'

'*No, we cannot*!' Benjamin tossed his serviette on to the table and stood up, then immediately sank back down into his chair with a look of pain. 'Oh my God, I'm about to have another heart attack,' he moaned, clutching his chest, and Corinna stood up, alarmed.

'Sit back down!' Antonio commanded. 'He's not about to have anything of the sort! It's just his way of trying to avoid the unavoidable.'

Benjamin banged his fists on the table and shouted, 'Will you stop shouting under my roof!'

Antonio sighed heavily, like a frustrated adult who was attempting to deal with a wayward child, and that only made his father angrier.

'Look, I merely think that it would do you good to get outside, instead of remaining cooped up in Deanbridge.'

'And how do you know that I don't free-foot it in London whenever I damn well please?'

'McBride.'

'The traitor,' Benjamin muttered forlornly. 'The spy. The Judas.'

Was there a flash of amusement in those silver depths? Corinna wondered. It was hard to tell because Antonio gave nothing away.

'What work is this that you're doing?'

Benjamin looked at his son, then hurriedly looked away and gave the question some thought. 'A historical piece on the house,' he said huffily, 'since you ask. I should be flattered, it's the first bit of interest you've expressed in my life for years, even if it *was* only prompted by you eavesdropping outside the kitchen door.

And no,' he addressed Corinna with the same lofty voice, 'I don't think I will go to any library today. I feel quite weak all of a sudden.' He stood up and headed for the door and she quickly stood up as well.

'Scared of me, are you?' Antonio murmured as she walked past him, and she froze in her tracks.

'Don't make me laugh!' she snapped back.

'Then sit down and finish your coffee.'

He wasn't looking at her. He was pouring himself some coffee, and she hesitated. She badly wanted to follow Benjamin, who had vanished in the direction of the study, but Antonio had thrown down the gauntlet, and a part of her had risen up in angry protest at the mocking challenge in his voice.

So he thought that she was scared of him, did he? She shrugged and sat back down.

Without Benjamin's presence, alone with Antonio, the kitchen suddenly seemed smaller and hotter than it had been before.

'I see the careful little bun is back in place,' he said, sweeping his eyes over her. 'You really look much better with your hair loose, though I must say the outfit is an improvement on that dismal thing you were wearing the last time I saw you.'

Corinna's eyes flared. '*This* is why I don't relish being in your company,' she bit out, 'and it has nothing to do with being *scared of you*. I just don't like being insulted constantly. There are better ways for me to fill my time.'

'Looking after my father? Working with him on this historical piece he's doing? Hardly absorbing for a young girl like you. How old are you anyway? Eighteen? Nineteen?'

He lifted his coffee cup to his lips and looked at her from over the rim.

'Twenty-three, if you must know,' she answered. 'And as a matter of fact, I do find it very absorbing.'

'Do you? Strange. What were you doing before?'

Corinna debated whether she should answer that. She didn't like his tone of voice. It was too—innocently conversational. She had become accustomed to the drawn swords and now this sudden cessation of warfare made her uneasy.

'I worked in the casualty department of a hospital,' she admitted, 'in London.'

'And you left that to come and work here?' He sounded amazed at that, as if she had told him that she had given up the chance of going to the moon because she had to wash her hair, and she threw him a defensive glare.

'You make it sound as though it's a crime to want a change of job.'

'Not a crime. Just surprising.'

'And now I expect I shall have to sit through another lecture on how that is one more piece of evidence of my sticking around your father because of his money? ''You left the casualty department of a large teaching hospital to come here? Of course, there must be a reason. Of course, the reason must have to do with money. Of course, Benjamin Silver's got a lot of that. Put two and two together—hmm—of course, you're a gold-digger!'''

She hadn't meant to arouse humour, but she had, and Antonio laughed out loud, throwing his head back, and she saw again how disturbingly sexy he was when that cold arrogance was not stamped on his face.

He was staring at her, his eyebrows raised in amusement and she smiled reluctantly. Her heartbeat had speeded up and the walls of the kitchen were definitely closing in. Or at least, it felt that way. And it was getting much hotter in here. Wasn't it? After all, she was positively perspiring.

'Am I wrong?' she asked, struggling to make everything shift back into focus.

'As a matter of fact, yes. I found it surprising because I can't understand why anyone would volunteer to go from a demanding job to a more restful one. Why?' She could see that he was still trying to figure her out. He had initially raged against her for being a gold-digger, but maybe, somewhere, doubts about that were beginning to take root. She wasn't, after all, what he had expected. Part of him, no doubt, still nursed the notion that she might be after his father's money, but another part was curious to find out, if that wasn't the reason for her presence here, then what was? 'I can't understand it,' he said, his grey eyes still fixed on her face, trying to prise open the doors to her mind. 'Unless it's a retreat.' His eyes narrowed on her as he considered this option. 'Is it? Have you come here to escape something? To lick your wounds in privacy like a wounded bear?'

Corinna didn't comment, even though she was startled and vaguely disturbed at the accuracy of his observation. Hadn't she strongly wanted to escape from the break-up of her relationship with Michael when she had accepted this job at Deanbridge House? Hadn't she suddenly realised that she needed some freedom from her mother, from the dull predictability of her life? And maybe the reason she had stayed on so contentedly was because in finding Benjamin she had found a father-substitute. The train of thought was crystal-clear and it shocked her to realise that Antonio Silver had been the one to throw it into focus.

'It mystifies me,' he said in a sardonic, accusatory voice. '*You* mystify me.'

'There's nothing exceptional about wanting a break from the rat-race.'

'Isn't there?' It was a rhetorical question. 'Coping with the rat-race, the sheer pressure of it, breeds success, and what is life without success?'

'I suspect,' she responded drily, 'that it can be pretty enjoyable.'

He looked at her blankly and she saw that he really couldn't comprehend that train of thought. He was built for success, she realised. He was ambitious and more than that he possessed a cleverness which was a combination of brains and street-wise sharpness. To imagine him as anything but successful was impossible, and she wondered whether this was good or bad. Maybe, she thought, it was just different. She had never met anyone like him before. Michael had been typically the boy next door, something of a plodder academically, a great believer in work being a necessary evil.

'Good grief,' he drawled, standing up, 'I do believe I've shocked you. You don't really think that the best things in life are free, do you?'

'Yes, I do,' Corinna said, and he raised his eyebrows in irony.

'Then you're a rare breed. Or else a very good actress.'

So back to square one, she thought, standing up, already on the defence. So much for that brief feeling of companionship. It had probably been an illusion, anyway. Men like Antonio Silver never made *companions*. They made opponents. Or lovers. Her mouth went dry.

He had stopped by the kitchen door and was looking down at her.

'Of course,' he murmured, not moving a muscle, 'I can think of one very pleasurable thing that's free.'

'Oh, yes?' she asked innocently, 'and what's that?' Walks along a deserted beach at twilight? Dancing under a moonlit sky? Sitting on the green grass on a hot summer day?

He was staring at her and she realised suddenly what he meant and it was none of those things. Making love. His eyes said it and she blushed furiously. She felt paralysed with confusion and was shocked to realise that her body was screaming out for him to reach out and touch her. She took a panicked step backwards and he laughed without humour.

'I can tell that you can think of it too,' he said lazily and that made her go an even brighter shade of red. 'And much as I'm tempted to demonstrate what I'm talking about,' he glanced at his watch, 'I have an appointment.'

The prosaic action broke the spell and she was furious with herself.

He gave her a brief nod and left. She heard his steps gradually fade, then the distant slam of the front door, and her body sagged as the tension left her.

He had been playing with her just then, amusing himself at her expense, and she had fallen for it, hook, line and sinker. The thought made her want to cringe in embarrassment.

The awful thing was that she had never, in a whole lifetime of dates and gentle necking, been as aware of Michael as a man as she had been of Antonio just then, for fifteen suffocating minutes. It was a thought which she didn't want to dwell too hard on, and she immediately headed for the study to find Benjamin. He would take her mind off what had just happened. He was reality; Antonio Silver and her reaction to him were not. She didn't like the man and there was no way that she would allow herself to give in, even momentarily, to that sudden rush of attraction she had felt in the kitchen, when his grey eyes had caressed her like a lazy, lingering fingertouch.

You're a rare breed, he had said, either that or a very good actress, and it didn't take a genius to work out that neither was to his personal liking. He was a sophisticated man whose appetite was more suited to the elegant women he doubtless entertained. What he felt for her would be either derision for the gold-digger or amusement for the *ingénue*, or else a combination of both.

Her expression was grim as she pushed open the study door and Benjamin, who was sitting at the desk with an assortment of books in front of him, looked up at her in surprise.

'Where have you been?' he asked, without any of the querulousness she had expected.

'Chatting to your son,' she said, with what she considered a huge understatement.

'You don't look as though it was a very pleasant chat.'

'It wasn't,' she said briefly.

'He can be a bit overpowering, I've discovered,' Benjamin said, with what sounded very much like grudging admiration to her ears. 'Too overpowering for this house! The sooner he's out, the better. I hope you told him that. He doesn't seem to pay a scrap of attention to what I have to say! He thinks that it would do me good to get out of the house, indeed! Why? So that he could treat it more like a hotel than he does already?'

'If he wanted to stay in a hotel,' Corinna said wryly, 'then I'm sure he would. Your son doesn't strike me as the sort of person who does anything unless he wants to.'

'Hard-headed,' Benjamin muttered, and she heard that unwilling paternal admiration in his voice again, even though she was quite sure that he wasn't aware of it. He began leafing through his books rapidly, and Corinna fell in easily enough, not inviting any further discussion of Antonio. Just talking about him made her skin prickle and that annoyed her intensely. And when she thought of how she had responded to that suggestion in his eyes, she felt even more annoyed, so she made sure that the day was filled with a thousand and one activities.

She was sure that he would not return before evening, hopefully long after she had retired to bed, but to her dismay the deep timbre of his voice in the hall, chatting to Edna, heralded his return as she and Benjamin were relaxing in the lounge with a pot of tea and the newspapers, several of which Benjamin had delivered daily to the house, and all of which he read voraciously, even though he refused to venture into the wide world.

He shot her a ferocious look and she had an insane desire to protest, But it's not my fault if he's returned at nine-thirty instead of midnight!

She could hear Edna giggling, of all things, and Benjamin raised his eyes skyward as he read her thoughts.

'Some guard dog *she* turned out to be!' he said, and Corinna grinned. 'She always did have a soft spot for my son. I was an idiot to think that time would have changed that.'

There were footsteps approaching and Antonio strode in with Edna following in his wake, with a spare cup and saucer in one hand and some home-made biscuits in the other.

She laid them out, fussing over their arrangement on the china plate, until Benjamin snapped irritably, 'They look fine, Edna! No need to spend the rest of the night fiddling with them. As far as I can see, we're not entertaining the Queen of England!'

'Oh, don't be so grumpy,' Edna returned with spirit, turning her attention to pouring Antonio a cup of tea. 'Master Silver's has a hard day, he tells me, he needs a little taking care of.'

Benjamin looked as though he didn't agree with that in the least and Corinna thought sourly, Taking care of? Do boa constrictors need taking care of after a hard day spent devouring innocent victims?

Antonio had discarded his jacket and he sat down and began cuffing the sleeves of his shirt.

'Please,' he said, once Edna had left the room, 'don't either of you two overwhelm me with your enthusiasm to learn what I've been doing all day.'

'What have you been doing all day?' Corinna obliged, since Benjamin was clearly not going to, and she didn't much feel like spending the remainder of the evening in an atmosphere of tense silence.

'I've been looking for premises for the company I'm planning on opening,' Antonio said, looking at his father who was concentrating on the newspaper on his lap.

'And along the way,' he continued evenly, 'I've found something of interest. Papa, I'm talking to you!'

Benjamin raised startled eyes and Corinna expected him to burst out in his usual display of anger, but the tone of Antonio's voice had obviously surprised him into temporary speechlessness.

'Don't you dare take that tone with me!' he said, after a long pause.

'Then at least pretend to be interested when I'm talking to you!' Their eyes met, both as fierce as the other, both oblivious of her presence in the room.

'I'm tired,' Benjamin muttered, standing up, 'I'm going to bed.' But this time Antonio wasn't backing down. There was angry determination in his eyes as he walked towards his father and gently propelled him back into the chair.

'Not,' he said, 'until you've seen what this thing of interest is that I've brought back with me. It's for you.'

Benjamin looked at his son suspiciously, but there was a glimmer of interest in his eyes now.

'For me? For me? Since when have you ever showered me with gifts?'

'Stay where you are,' Antonio said, ignoring the sarcasm, 'I'll be right back. It's in the car.'

He left the room and Benjamin turned to Corinna, his blue eyes bright and alive. *He loves having his son in this house,* she thought with sudden insight. *He complains constantly about it, but he loves having him around, because he prefers the fighting to the absence.*

'This is ridiculous,' he said to her, clasping his fingers together. 'What could he have bought that would be of any interest to me? Answer me that!'

'I have no idea,' Corinna admitted. 'And much as I'd love to stay and see, I really think I'll retire to bed now.'

'Oh, no, you don't.'

'You have to face him on your own some time.'

'Not if I can help it.'

For the first time, that really irritated her, not because it indicated bossiness on Benjamin's part, but because she was discovering that she functioned far better when Antonio was not around.

It was too late to run now, though. They both heard him returning, and when he reappeared it was with a huge box in his arms. He deposited it on the ground and began stripping off the tape around it.

Benjamin was staring at this in fascination, like a child looking at a Christmas tree, and she felt a pang of real sorrow for him. All those years in this huge house, surrounded by the very finest that money could buy, and lacking the one thing that money couldn't: his son.

When all the tape had been removed, Antonio flapped back the lid of the box and reached inside for its contents.

'Just what I've always wanted,' Benjamin said drily. 'It should look just dandy in the corner of the room, over there, underneath the Seurat.'

'You have a way with words, Papa,' Antonio said with the sort of fond exasperation that Benjamin sometimes inspired. He was unaware of the tone of his voice, but Corinna wasn't. She looked at that dark, averted head and thought that this was the first time that they had not been sparring at each other.

'It's a computer,' Antonio said, setting it down on the table in front of Benjamin, who looked at it with bafflement.

'You bought me a computer. How thoughtful.'

Antonio grinned, and Corinna smiled too because she was enjoying this unique display of familiarity between the two of them. How long it would last, she had no idea, but everything had its beginning and perhaps this was the beginning of a truce.

'What am I supposed to do with it?' Benjamin asked, still staring at the grey screen with its smooth ivory keyboard as if it were an alien which had suddenly fallen out of the sky and on to his coffee-table.

'You're supposed to help me with it,' Antonio said gravely, and they looked at each other.

'Help you do what?' Benjamin asked, and Corinna heard the defensive tone back in his voice with a sinking heart. Well, it couldn't last, could it, that brief, affectionate interlude? Now Antonio would get his back up as well, more terse exchanges, and then one or the other or both would end up storming out of the room.

'I'm opening a subsidiary of my pharmaceutical company over here,' Antonio explained. 'I have subsidiaries all over Europe. England is the last bastion to fall. It's basically going to be a distribution outfit, but I'll need someone to be in overall charge.'

'And where do I fit in?' Benjamin barked.

'Well, you're damned clever and it's time you stopped burying yourself in this house.'

Immediately Benjamin frowned. 'So it's pity, then, is it? I'm an old man to be humoured and pitied. I suppose that fool Angus has put you up to this? Is that it?'

'No,' Antonio said with an impatient shake of his head, 'that's not it.'

'I won't have anything to do with some hocus-pocus so-called job which you've engineered because you've decided to remember my existence and you're feeling sorry for me. No, thanks!'

'You'll have to learn how to operate this animal, of course,' Antonio said, disregarding the outburst. 'Do you know anything at all about computers?'

'I'm an old fool,' Benjamin said tartly, 'or so you think. How could I possibly know anything about computers?'

'You'll have to learn. Nothing too technical. Just the basics.'

'I'm not taking your job!'

'It shouldn't take long. You have the sort of brain that would be able to grasp it quite easily, I should have imagined.'

'How would you know what sort of brain I have? You haven't been around for years! The bloody postboy probably knows my brain better than you do!'

'Of course, you'll be working with other people, but this computer will give you the freedom to do most of your stuff right here from the house. Everything you need to know will be accessible at the touch of a finger. However, if you're scared to accept the challenge...'

'Don't be impertinent, my boy!' Benjamin roared. 'But you're sadly mistaken if you think that you can steam-roller me into doing something I don't want to do!'

'Give it some thought,' Antonio said carefully, and Benjamin stood up with a snort that could have meant anything.

He left the room and Antonio turned to Corinna and said, 'What do you think that meant?'

'That he'll think about it.'

'I thought so, but I couldn't be sure.'

She began to leave and he stopped her, with his hand on her arm. She stiffened immediately and he said, in a cooler voice, 'Oh, yes, I forgot that you don't like the caveman approach.' He dropped his hand and walked across to the bar, which was a sleek walnut affair in the corner of the room. Benjamin kept it stocked with a few bottles, even though he didn't drink much and his visitors were few and far between. Antonio asked her whether she cared for a nightcap and when she shook her head he poured himself a large gin and tonic, then he sat back on the sofa with his legs stretched out in front of him and half closed his eyes. Even in repose, it was impossible to miss the long, powerful lines of his body. The suit which he was wearing had the impeccable cut of something that had cost a great deal of money, and it accentuated the lithe hardness of his physique. She found herself staring at him and wondering about his private life. Was there one woman in particular, or was he resting between affairs? He didn't strike her as the sort who relished a life of celibacy, but on the other hand she hadn't been aware of him locking himself away somewhere and phoning Italy on a daily basis. He probably didn't have to do that, though, she thought with a trace of acidity; he probably had a queue of women panting behind him whether he lifted a phone to call them or not.

She realised, with a little start, that he was watching her, and she said in a rush, 'Where have you decided for your company? You must have been very successful if you've found the ideal spot in the space of one day. I know it's nothing like looking for a house, but I know people who have spent months looking for just the right place!' She was babbling, like a fool, to cover her attack of awkwardness.

'Sit down,' he said, then added as an afterthought, 'please. It's more relaxing talking to someone who isn't hovering as though she might turn tail and run away at any minute.'

'Well, only for a minute,' Corinna said, perching alongside him on the sofa.

'Why? Have you got plans to spend the remainder of the night out on the tiles?'

'I like to get to bed at a decent hour,' she said, 'and I want to do a spot of reading ...' Really riveting stuff, she thought, I sound like Miss Boring of the Year, not that it matters one way or another what he thinks. 'So where did you find?' she asked, switching to her original question.

'A building just about ten miles from here, as a matter of fact,' Antonio said, swallowing some of his drink and not taking his eyes off her face. 'And no, it wasn't as difficult as you think. I have people over here who had done quite a bit of groundwork, so I only had to check out a few places. The one I chose is an eighteenth-century house which has been converted into office space. It's precisely the right size.'

'How lucky for you.'

'I don't believe in luck,' Antonio said, his lips twisting. 'In life, people make their own luck. I have no time for those people who spend their time blaming life, the weather, the government, everything under the sun, for their misfortunes.'

'So you're a very tolerant person, then?' Corinna asked sweetly, and he smiled, another of those relaxed, charming smiles that made her breath catch.

Dangerous. That was what her mind was telling her. Sitting here, alone, at night, with Antonio Silver, was dangerous. Oh not because he might jump on her or anything like that, but because she was putting herself in a situation where her emotions were in turmoil. Those silver-grey eyes threw her off course, especially when they were staring at her, which they were right now. She would do well to remember that this man, charm or no charm, didn't trust her.

'I like to think I'm fair,' he said, getting up to pour himself another drink. 'Sure you won't join me?'

'Thank you but no.'

'It might interfere with your reading?'

She wondered whether he was being sarcastic, even though his voice was serious enough.

'It might,' she agreed easily, thinking that now was as good a time to head for the door as any.

'And what else do you do? Apart from reading, that is?'

'Quite a lot, actually,' she said defensively. 'I keep in touch with all my friends at the weekends. I don't spend my life glued to books.'

'I never suggested that you did,' he murmured, sipping from his glass and looking at her as though she were a curious exhibit of some sort. Which she supposed she was, for a man like him. He circled the rim of the glass with one long finger and then said casually, 'And in between all these hectic activities, do you get time to see men? Or is my father the only man in your life?'

She didn't like the way he said that. It was the sort of question that, taken at face value, was no more than an amusing observation, but she knew better than to take anything he said at face value.

'I see we're back to this,' she snapped, leaning forward and looking at him.

'Back to what?'

'Back to your grand theory on my cultivating your father for his money!'

'Why else are you here, then?' he threw at her.

'Why does it matter? Isn't it enough for me to tell you that I'm not after your father's precious money?'

'No, dammit!' The vehemence of his reply surprised them both. She watched as the mocking self-composure returned, then he looked at her from under his lashes and she felt a little unsteady. He filled the room, she realised, obliterating everything in it. When he was around, it was impossible to think, to see, anything or anyone else.

'I don't like mysteries,' he said softly, cradling his glass between his hands.

'And I don't like being an open book.'

'The only people who say that are those people who have something to hide. What are you hiding? A broken love-life?'

She flushed and he smiled slowly, satisfied.

'So that's it, is it? What went wrong?'

'That's none of your business.'

'Couldn't he put up with that temper of yours?'

Corinna stood up, shaking and he got to his feet just as quickly, covering the distance between them before she had time to take to her heels and flee.

He towered over her, tall, dark, imposing, his eyes glinting with a warm curiosity that sent the blood rushing to her head. They were only inches apart. His clean, masculine smell filled her nostrils until she felt faint.

'Were you in love with the man? You can't run away from things, if that's why you're here.'

'I am not *running away*! I'm recovering. Anyway, this is no business of yours.'

'So you already said. Tell me about him.'

She half turned and he reached out, his hand flicking to catch her wrist.

'There's nothing to tell!' she said angrily, tossing her head like a trapped horse.

'There's always something to tell. *Everyone* has something to tell. Have you stayed on here because my father is soothing after this boyfriend, lover, whatever, of yours?'

Michael? Her lover? The thought almost brought a smile to her lips.

'No one is worth weeping over,' Antonio said, misinterpreting her silence. 'Love is an illusion and as for sex...' His voice trailed off and she looked up into that dark, handsome face and her head began to swim. He was still holding her wrist, but the pressure of his fingers was different now, more something of a subtle caress.

Suddenly the air seemed charged with unspoken tension. Then what he did next was so totally unexpected that she was shocked into not responding. He released her and instead softly, gently, touched her breast, a light, feathery touch that sent a bolt of white hot heat searing through her.

He didn't make any move to kiss her. He just stood there and continued to look at her, deep into her eyes, while his hand aroused her body to a pitch of breathless excitement, the like of which she had never experienced before. She could feel the heavy ache of her breasts as they responded to him, could feel her body going limp and moist.

Her brain felt sluggish and her cheeks were burning.

It took an enormous effort to say, as calmly and as coldly as she could, 'There's nothing that you could tell me about sex. It isn't a game that people play.' His hand had dropped, but she could still feel the burning eroticism of his touch. 'Not me, anyway.' She tried to sound disdainful but to her own ears she sounded croaky and uncontrolled, which was just how she felt.

'Of course not,' he said, and she didn't like the look of the smile that slowly curved his mouth.

She walked towards the door, pausing only when she heard his voice from behind her.

'Have an exciting weekend, by the way,' he said, and there was a thread of amusement in his voice. 'Don't over-exhaust yourself.'

She didn't answer. She would have dearly loved to respond with some equally ironic quip, but she couldn't. These sort of urbane word games weren't her style at all.

It was only later, in her bedroom, that she realised what she should have done. She should have put him on the spot by turning the tables on him. She should have quizzed him about his damn life! Next time, she promised. Next time she wouldn't let herself be rattled into silence. Next time she wouldn't let her body misbehave without her permission.

# CHAPTER FOUR

As it turned out, Corinna had a fraught weekend. The image of Antonio clung to her mind with unwelcome tenacity and all the good common sense in the world couldn't conceal the horrendous fact that she was attracted to him. The whole thing baffled her. How could she be attracted to a man like that? she wondered. True, he was very good-looking, in the literal sense of the word, all black-haired and grey-eyed and with that brand of steely self-confidence that some women swooned over, but which, when she sat down and thought about it coolly and rationally, was not her kind of thing at all.

Dear sweet Michael, she had thought at one point, why couldn't she have fallen in love with him? A lot could have been avoided if she had. For a start, she would never have found herself at Deanbridge House, and she would never have come into contact with Antonio Silver.

If only all her sensible plans hadn't come a cropper at the last moment. Michael was thoughtful, kind and not unattractive. He would make any woman a fine husband, as her mother had contentedly pointed out to her on numerous occasions. And much more than that, he was safe. She could, she had thought at the time, marry him and never have to fear the turbulence that came from more fiery relationships. She had spent her childhood living with turbulence and it had been too much like treading in a minefield for her voluntarily to repeat the experience when it came to settling down with a man.

And how easy it had been for their casual friendship to become a habit, and for that habit to become an engagement. Nothing positive had really ever been said, it was more that nothing negative had been spoken. Michael, with his teaching job, had wanted her safety just as much as she had wanted his, and they had just found themselves drifting into a mutual decision to tie the knot. No proposal, just a steady slide towards what had seemed to them both inevitable.

Breaking off their engagement had been the really first bit of true self-assertion that she had ever shown, and she could see now why her mother had been shocked and alarmed. She was a dominating personality, happy to have her daughter living peaceably in her shadow. Her marriage to Michael would not have jeopardised that.

But that flash of independence had frightened her, and Corinna, from a distance and with time on her side, could sympathise with that for, with all her mother's faults, she was, after all, still her mother, struggling against the prospect of ageing, baulking at the wrinkles on her face. Perhaps, Corinna thought, more dependent on me than she would ever have voiced.

Deanbridge House. What a haven that had been. To throw in the rigours of a job that was draining her, to escape the complexities of her broken relationship and her mother's accusatory reminders that she was giving up a wonderful man, had been blissful. But Antonio, she thought, irritated to find him springing back into her thoughts, had been right when he had said that when it came to running out on yourself, there was no place to hide.

It was late evening by the time she finally made it back to the house and Benjamin, to her amazement, was still up. On a Sunday he was accustomed to retiring to bed early to watch a bit of television and attack the *Sunday Times*.

Corinna walked into the study, however, to find him alert and wide awake and devouring a computer manual.

'I haven't said that I'm taking that damned job,' he growled, following her eyes to the manual.

'Have you had a good weekend?' Corinna chose to ask, sitting on the edge of the desk with her hands tucked under her thighs. Where's your son? she wanted to ask, not relishing the prospect of him bursting through the door unexpectedly.

'So-so.' He shrugged and flapped the computer manual on to the desk.

'What did you get up to?'

'This and that.'

'So-so? This and that?' She laughed. 'You're being particularly secretive this evening.'

Benjamin raised his eyes sheepishly to hers. 'Well, as a matter of fact, Antonio's been his usual overbearing self. Telling me all about this damned job as if it's a foregone conclusion that I'm going to accept it. Which it isn't.'

'No.'

'We also talked about other things.' There was a long silence and she wondered whether he was going to continue or not. 'I may have been a bit hard on him, I admit, but I'm not saying that I was wrong.' Another pause. 'It's just that twelve years ago, when he was nineteen and fresh out of university, I asked him whether he would consider taking over the reins of handling my properties and he chose to decline. He chose to fly to his mother's side and take over the pharmaceutical company. Can you blame me if I was put out? I had done everything for that boy and he deserted me!'

'Oh.'

'It transpires that my ex-wife, Claudia, was ill and the firm was dissolving because of bad management. He says now that he wasn't going to stay on there, but it was worse than he had thought and he found himself trapped into getting it back together, but he never said anything about that at the time—oh, no, the next thing he did was to storm over here accusing me of all sorts of things! The damned cheek!' He was beginning to look flushed and flustered, and Corinna said quickly, 'Please don't carry on, not if you don't want to. You mustn't get yourself worked up over the past.'

'Don't start philosophising again! I want to talk about it anyway. It's been locked inside for too long.' He sighed an old man's sigh and continued quietly, 'Claudia had apparently told him that the reason she left me was because I had been having an affair. He stormed over here and of course I refused to discuss it. I hadn't been having any damned affair but I saw no reason to launch into squalid explanations. I asked him at the time whether he thought I was capable of being adulterous and we got into the most almighty row about the whole thing.' He was reliving the episode. She could see it in the faraway look in his eyes and she suddenly wished that she wasn't listening to all this; this was private stuff. But he was determined to finish and she remained where she was. 'He flew back to Italy and that was the last that I saw of him.'

'He didn't keep in touch at all.'

Benjamin glanced at her sheepishly once again. 'He might have. To start with, but he had cut me to the quick.'

'You were proud,' she said quietly, and he glared at her.

'If a man hasn't got pride, then what has he got? Anyway, we talked about all this and it seems that

Claudia lied about me as a ploy to turn my son, *my own son*, against me.'

'So now that you've reconciled, will you be accepting his offer of the job?'

'Don't you rush to assumptions, my girl!' Benjamin said tartly. 'I just happened to peruse that manual because I wasn't sleepy.' The computer had been deposited on the desk and plugged in and he looked at the screen suspiciously. 'I suppose tomorrow we might see our way to tinkering with that damned great thing, but not because I'm taking any job from my son, just out of curiosity, you understand.'

'I understand.' On impulse, she bent down and kissed the top of his head and it was then that she saw Antonio out of the corner of her eye, a dark presence by the doorframe. She felt her body freeze for a fraction of a minute, then she straightened and said lightly,                          '

'You have company, so if you'll excuse me.'

Benjamin looked up and saw Antonio and out of habit he glowered at the powerful shape, then he waved at them both. 'You're excused, you're excused, you both are. This is my study and I'm here doing some reading, so off you both go. Talk to each other, compare weekends, discuss the weather, but just let me get on with this. I'll take myself off to bed and you needn't worry,' he added, looking at Corinna, 'that I'll forget those tablets. I'll remember to take them with some water, so you can forget your nurse's cap for the moment.' He turned back to the manual, ignoring their presence, and Corinna eased herself off the desk and reluctantly made her way to the door.

She didn't want to meet Antonio's eyes, but as she brushed past him her body felt as though it were on fire. He shut the door quietly behind her and then turned to her, and with a jolt of alarm she saw that he was angry, enraged in fact, fuming. His eyes were ablaze and his features were set into a hard, forbidding mask.

'Is something the matter?' She stumbled over the words, bewildered.

'Is something the matter? You dare ask that!' He pressed her back against the wall, pinning her there with his hands, then he glanced at the closed study door and hissed, 'Come with me.'

'I won't!' But he was dragging her along to the lounge while she struggled against him, breathing heavily, her hair, for once loose, swinging around her face.

Once they were in the lounge, he closed the door, still with one hand on her and then swung her round to face him. 'What the hell was *that* all about?' he asked savagely.

'What are you talking about?'

'I go to the kitchen to pour myself a cup of coffee and, hearing voices from the study, I decide to go and find out what's going on and what do I find? You kissing my father! Did you decide to don the lover's cap the minute you thought it was safe? Did you think that there was no need to be careful since you didn't think that I was around? Is that it?'

She would have slapped him, hard, if she had been able to, but her arms were locked in his hands.

'Yes!' she said in a high, angry voice. 'I decided to don the lover's cap. How clever you are to spot that!'

She shouldn't have said that. She knew that immediately; now was not the time for off-the-cuff quips.

'What is going on here? Tell me! I want the truth!' He shook her and she kicked him on the shin, a spontaneous action which immediately had the desired effect. He released her and staggered back on to the sofa with a grimace of pain.

Corinna stood rubbing her arms and glaring at him. 'I gave your father a peck on his head, a gesture of affection, and that's the truth—take it or leave it.' From this distance and with him safely immobilised for the time being on the sofa, it was much easier to be calm. She was still trembling, though, and although she wasn't sorry about having kicked him on the shin, she was a little aghast at her action. She had never done *anything* remotely like that in her entire life. The man brought out a side of her which she had never even known existed.

He looked at her from under his lashes and his expression was a little less savage now. 'You could have said that without resorting to physical violence.' He pulled up his trousers and looked at his leg. 'I've known a lot of passionate women in my time, but I've never been kicked by any of them.'

He continued rubbing his leg and she said in a more collected voice, 'I was angry. I don't like being accused of something that's simply not true.'

'I suppose I should be grateful there wasn't a golf club lying around. You might have taken it to my head.'

'Is it very painful?' Corinna asked, taking a few tentative steps towards him and peering at the leg in question. She, personally, couldn't see much wrong with it.

'Yes,' Antonio muttered darkly, 'damn painful.'

'So were your fingers pressing into my arms.' She was standing over him now, looking down, with her hair on either side of her face like a white curtain.

Their eyes met and she looked away nervously.

'Look,' he commanded, pointing to his shin. 'What do you see?'

'A foot.'

'There!' He jabbed at his shin. 'There.'

She sat down next to him and peered at where he was indicating. 'It does look a bit bruised,' she admitted. 'I suppose I ought to get a compress and see to it.'

'You *are* a nurse; it's the least you could do.'

Corinna dutifully dampened a rag and returned to the lounge with it. It was all unnecessary, of course. He was making a mountain out of a molehill, she thought, and acting as though he were the victim when in fact none of this would have happened if he hadn't over-reacted to a perfectly innocent situation.

She pressed the damp cloth against his skin and tried to ignore what his proximity was doing to her pulse rate. Being attracted to him was like playing with fire, and that was a dangerous game. She could feel the warmth of his body through the cold compress and she wondered whether that was her imagination playing tricks on her, trying to trip her up.

'There,' she said briskly. 'I think you'll live to see another day.'

'Is that it? Shouldn't it be bandaged?'

'Don't be ridiculous. There's a slight bruise, if that, not an open gaping wound.'

'Some bedside manner,' Antonio muttered, shrugging down his trouser leg and reclining back on the sofa from where he proceeded to look at her through half closed eyes. 'I feel sorry for all those casualty victims who happened to find themselves in your ward. I suppose you just looked them up and down, ordered them to stop feeling sorry for themselves and informed them that they were wasting valuable bed space.'

'I did not!' Corinna said heatedly. 'I happen to be very sympathetic, when the situation demands. I just think that a minuscule bruise is nothing to get too worked up about!'

'Relax. It was just a joke,' he said softly. 'I know you do a good job. I have it on reliable evidence from my father who sings your praises loud and long, in between telling me that I'm an ingrate who broke his heart and can't expect forgiveness.'

He smiled and it was as if he had never been that angry, aggressive man who had hauled her along the corridor less than half an hour before. That was one of those dangerous things about him, though, wasn't it? That easy ability to captivate, to make you go along with him, to mesmerise you. He hurled his insults then, when he was through, he smiled that persuasive, sensual smile of his and took it for granted that you would be charmed.

Corinna sat back and primly pressed her hands along her skirt. She had no intention of being charmed.

'At least he's talking to you,' she said, linking her fingers together and resting them on her lap. 'That's an improvement on his initial reaction, isn't it?'

'Isn't it just?' Something soft and lazy in his voice sent alarm bells ringing in her head, warning her to keep her eyes averted because to meet his might be a big mistake. She was aware of him though. His powerful body, clad in dark trousers and jumper, the strong forearms, the long, muscular legs casually extended in front of him. He radiated dark vitality. Even if she had had her eyes tightly closed she would have still felt it sweeping over her.

'He told me that you discussed your business proposition with him in great detail.'

'I did,' Antonio murmured. 'He seems to think that I've created the opening through some sense of misguided and long-delayed guilt, which couldn't be further from the truth, although I have to confess that I'm sorry I didn't come over sooner to patch things up between us.' He folded his arms and watched her watching him.

'No, well, I wasn't here, was I?' Corinna responded bluntly, lifting her eyes to meet his and then wishing she hadn't. 'I mean,' she continued hastily, reddening, 'your main reason for flying over here was to throw me out of this house, wasn't it?'

He shrugged, not taking his eyes off her face. He seemed, she noticed, to have completely forgotten about his shin, despite the almighty fuss he had made of it a short while ago.

'It did seem an opportune moment,' Antonio admitted, 'but I would have come nevertheless. I had this business to take care of, and to be frank, I had come to the conclusion that too many years had been wasted because of pride, for which I blame myself as well as my father.'

'Like father, like son.'

'You think so?' He laughed under his breath, a disconcertingly sexy sound that made the hairs on the back of her neck stand on end, and sent a shiver of electric awareness through her. 'Perhaps you'd like to give me a little affectionate kiss as well, in that case?'

He was flirting! She couldn't believe it. She had convinced herself that she was about as much his type as he was hers, despite what had happened between them on the Friday evening, yet here he was, flirting. Was it because she was the only woman around and he needed to flex his sexual muscles? Or maybe after that last incident between them, when surely the response of her body to his fingers had told its own story, whatever her protests to the contrary, he now saw her as easy game. Whatever the reason, she couldn't prevent the flare of dreadful excitement that shot through her, even though she did her best to staunch it.

'Now I've scared you,' he said in a humble voice that reeked of laughter. 'You'll turn tail and run, I expect, the way you did before. How was your weekend, by the way?'

'Fine.' Her voice, she was relieved to hear, at least did not betray the strangling confusion that was sweeping through her. She sounded calm and normal.

'Was it? Glad to be out of here? Did you miss my father?'

'I always miss him when I go away, I'm fond of him.'

'And what about me? Missed me?' He looked at her through half-closed eyes and she returned a serene look.

Sophisticated verbal games, she reminded herself. That was what all this was about. He was toying with her, enjoying her embarrassment. She had to steer him, in a similarly sophisticated manner, away from the subject of this, and on to something altogether less threatening. But how was she supposed to do that? she wondered. To launch suddenly into a string of observations on the pleasant weather would have added fuel to his amusement.

'No,' she said, after a while. 'Why should I?'

He frowned at that answer, and she saw that he was taken aback by her refusal to be provoked.

'Very cool and collected this evening, aren't you? I prefer it when you drop that controlled, businesslike act and show me some of that fire inside you.'

'Well, I do apologise,' Corinna said steadily, 'but you're out of luck.'

That made him frown more and she offered a polite smile.

It was an effort, though. He was so close to her, she realised. With her body turned to his, her knees were almost touching his thigh, and it wouldn't take much of an effort on his part to reach out towards her.

'You never did tell me why you broke up with your boyfriend,' he murmured, unfolding his arms, and leaning back against the sofa to clasp them behind his head. Was he aware, she wondered, of the sensuality of his movements? He must be, she decided.

'No,' Corinna replied placidly, 'I didn't, did I? In fact, I do believe I told you at the time that it was none of your business.'

He was beginning to look a little irritated.

'You're damned secretive.'

'No more than average. I'm sure you would be as unwilling to discuss your private life with me as I am with you. It's just that I don't choose to quiz you about it. It's none of my business, and anyway...' She smiled and her smile implied the unspoken rider that she wasn't interested enough in him to ask questions.

His brows met in a black line and his irritation became more apparent.

'I am trying damned hard with you,' he said heavily, leaning forward and resting his elbows on his knees. 'You complain that I accused you unfairly of being a gold-digger. Now that I'm encouraging you to explain why you're here, you refuse to answer.'

'Oh——' she raised wide, surprised eyes to his '—is that what you're doing? Giving me a chance to explain myself? How considerate of you. I apologise for being boorish by refusing to oblige.'

His brows again met in an angry scowl. 'You probably scared him to death. He probably thought that he was getting a neat, quiet, orderly blonde, and then discovered that there was a raging tiger underneath, waiting to get out.'

'No, he did not!' Corinna snapped, drawn into a position of self-defence, despite her good intentions. 'Michael and I just discovered that we were not suited! In fact, *I* was the one who made the decision to end the relationship!' She saw him smile, and realised with an inward groan that he had got just what he had wanted.

'Michael,' he murmured. 'Uninspiring name. Dull, was he?'

She ignored that and continued speaking as if she hadn't been interrupted. 'Not that you are anyone to judge relationships. For a start, you're hardly the family man with a long, contented marriage behind you.'

He shrugged and his eyes glinted. 'Alas, no marriage, but,' he added, 'quite a bit of contentment.'

'Really?' she said, trying to sound bored. Her heart was beating wildly, though.

'Really.' He reached out and stroked her arm with one finger, a slow, intimate gesture that sent her senses reeling. She was assaulted by the same choking feeling of panic that had hit her the last time he had chosen to touch her, and she snatched her arm away as if she had been burnt.

'Scared?' he taunted softly, with a little smile.

'I'm not afraid of you. I thought I'd told you that before.' She wasn't taking any chances, though. She had inched back along the sofa, making sure that her body was positioned as far away from his as was physically possible.

'So you did.'

There was a long silence, during which she tried desperately to get herself back into order, and she was about to say something, *anything*, to change the subject, when there was a sharp knock on the door and at the same time the telephone in the adjoining room shrieked into life. Saved by not one bell but two.

She heard him swear under his breath and he shouted, 'Come in!' at which point Benjamin strolled in, looking at them both suspiciously.

'I hope I haven't interrupted anything?' he asked with his eyebrows raised and Corinna said with enormous relief, 'Of course not!' The phone was still ringing in the background, and she continued, still flustered, 'I'll just get the telephone, if you'll both excuse me.'

She fled. Her skin felt as if it were on fire and she couldn't imagine what Benjamin was thinking. He was old, true enough, but he wasn't stupid, and he must have noticed that she was not entirely in control of herself when she confronted him. What would be going through his head?

At least she had not given in to Antonio, though. At least she hadn't been that stupid. She was honest enough, however, to admit to herself that it had been a close thing. That yearning she had felt had been restrained only with enormous effort. The suffocating desire which she had felt for him had become, she realised with horror, a monstrous beast rearing up to break the chains which her rationality had imposed. And that frightened her. She just *couldn't* be feeling this way, not about Antonio Silver, who was the last man in the world she should be drawn to. She had spent a lifetime being sensible, pursuing a sensible career. How could this happen?

By the time she picked up the telephone she was ready to shout in frustration, or kick herself for her stupidity, or just simply to burst into tears.

'Yes,' she said, then in a more normal voice she went through the routine of rattling off Benjamin's number and then adding, in her most formal voice, 'may I help you?'

'I suppose you may.'

Corinna had no idea who would be calling at this hour of the night when she had gone to answer the telephone, and the woman's voice on the other end only plunged her into more bewilderment.

'Who would you like to talk to?' she asked, wondering how Benjamin had managed to keep a woman secret and, from the sound of the voice, a particularly exotic one. Did he sneak off late at night and paint the town red, while she idly imagined that he was safely tucked up under the duvet cover, sleeping the sleep of the good and righteous?

'Antonio Silver.'

Ah, Corinna thought acidly, as the jigsaw began to slot into shape. Never mind Benjamin and his mystery love-life. This woman was calling for his son, and she should have guessed that immediately because the voice carried the unmistakable strains of an accent, although the English was impeccable.

'And you are?' Corinna asked, out of a mixture of habit and curiosity.

'No one that could concern you, my dear. Now would you just run along and fetch Antonio for me if he's in? I know he'll be wide awake.' There was a throaty little chuckle from down the line. 'His batteries—how shall I put this?—run at full power at night.'

# CHAPTER FIVE

THERE was nothing that Corinna could say to that, and anyway no answering remark was expected. The woman, name withheld, obviously knew Antonio in a much wider capacity than friend alone, and had no desire to keep that information to herself.

'It's for you,' Corinna said bluntly, walking back into the lounge.

'Who is it? Antonio asked.

'I have no idea.' I could, she thought sourly, narrow it down to gender, but I don't suppose that would go a long way to your figuring out who the caller is. She's probably one in a line of many. 'She didn't wish to give her name.'

He vanished into the parlour, closing the door behind him, and she heard the low murmur of his voice with dislike.

'You should really be in bed,' she said to Benjamin, forcing herself to smile and appear as normal as possible, even though she was seething with a mixture of dislike for Antonio, disgust at herself, and general, unfocused confusion going on inside her. 'It's way past your bedtime.'

'Not to mention yours,' he retaliated, but with a humorous smile. 'Would you mind walking me up?'

'Of course not.' She took his arm, her mind jumping back to Antonio, the woman on the end of the phone, and what they were talking about, and she had to tell herself sternly that wasting time thinking about him would not do, not at all.

81

'So,' Benjamin said, 'how was your weekend? I never asked. Was it good?'

'Lovely, thank you.'

'It's just that you seem a little strained at the moment.' He allowed enough of a pause to avoid the accusation of being nosy, and then continued in the same fatherly voice, which didn't fool Corinna one bit, 'I do hope that son of mine hasn't been having a shouting match with you.'

'Oh no, not at all,' she said airily. 'Would you like me to fetch you up a cup of cocoa or will you take your tablets with water?'

'Water. It's just that you both seemed a bit bothered when I entered the lounge earlier on.'

They were at the top of the stairs now and she couldn't make it fast enough to Benjamin's bedroom. He was prying shamelessly, knowing quite well that the most she would do would be to try and evade his line of questioning.

He was taking his time, though, shuffling along as though he had all the time in the world to kill.

'As though,' he said, 'I had interrupted something.' Another polite pause. 'But if you say you weren't arguing, then I shall take your word for it, my dear.'

'How generous of you,' Corinna said drily.

Almost at the bedroom door, but not quite.

'And now that you've seen a bit more of him,' Benjamin said, unperturbed by her brief answers to his questions, 'what do you think of him? Quite the lady-killer, wouldn't you say?'

'I suppose some ladies would think so,' she murmured obligingly, knowing that her constant skirting around his questions was making him impatient.

'And you, my dear, are not one of them?'

She opened the bedroom door and hustled him in, laughing as she did so.

'Not at all. But I'm sure he has his admirers.'

'The woman on the telephone who refused to give her name, for example?'

'For example,' she agreed, pulling back his covers and patting the mattress in a meaningful manner. 'I shall leave your tablets for you, which I trust you will take before you go to sleep.'

'Oh, yes, yes, of course.' He brushed aside that matter with the dismissive gesture of someone flapping away a fly. 'This woman on the phone, did she say what she was to Antonio?'

Corinna sighed, but help was in sight. She walked towards the door purposefully and said in a firm voice, 'I spent maybe a minute on the telephone. Surprisingly enough, I didn't glean a great deal.'

'I wonder who she is,' Benjamin mused invitingly.

'I wonder.'

'Do you? Yes, I suppose he has got someone in his life. Of course, he's never mentioned anything to me, but that's not surprising. He's only just seen fit to darken this house; he's hardly going to step through the front door and immediately launch into his personal history for my benefit, is he? After all, I'm only his father.'

'And after all, you did do your utmost to turn him out,' Corinna couldn't resist murmuring with a smile.

'There is that,' Benjamin admitted magnanimously.

'I take it that all's well that ends well?'

'You take it wrong, my dear!' he informed her in a lordly voice, as she deposited his tablets on the bedside table and poured him a glass of water. 'How can I be expected to forget the past?'

'But you're no longer convinced that you're a prisoner in your own home until he leaves.'

'Are you cross-examining me, young lady?' he enquired huffily, and she shook her head. 'Of course I've seen my way to dispensing forgiveness. I won't have anyone saying that I'm small-minded.'

Corinna did her best not to burst out laughing at that.

'And have you made up your mind on the job?'

Benjamin looked away and said casually, 'I might give it a try. Antonio might well be offended if I turn down his offer, you know. Now, perhaps you'd better run along. It's late and you don't want to be walking about tomorrow with bags under your eyes. And before you go, I think that we might have a look at the local library tomorrow. We can get Tom to drive us in.'

Tom was Edna's husband. He was quite accustomed to using Benjamin's Rolls-Royce to run errands, but the times that he had been called upon to drive it in the capacity of chauffeur for Benjamin were so few and far between that Corinna wondered whether he wouldn't just collapse on the spot with amazement when he learnt that he would be taking passengers out in it. Since all he ever did in it was transport groceries, he had probably come to the conclusion that the Rolls was just an expensive version of a supermarket trolley.

'Good idea,' she said, nodding. 'We can have some lunch out, if you like, in a pub, perhaps.'

'We don't want to overdo things,' Benjamin said hastily, then he added, 'though that sounds like a damn fine idea, provided I can have a glass of something stronger than fruit juice.'

'We'll see.'

She stood at the door and he waved her away. He was in a good humour. She didn't imagine for a moment that he would be rushing around, fussing over Antonio and playing the dutiful parent, now that they were on the road to reconciliation, that wasn't his style. He would continue being gruff and direct, and no doubt they would forever more have their heated arguments about something or other, but they would also inspire one another.

As she strolled back to her bedroom, she wondered what Benjamin's wife had been like, then she wondered what the mysterious woman on the other end of the phone was like. Then, her hands clenched, she found her line of thoughts drifting back to the inevitable. What had happened between herself and Antonio in the lounge.

She didn't want to think about all that. She wanted to put it to the back of her mind where it could happily be consigned to cobwebs and eventual oblivion. Nothing in her life, though, not all the stiff lectures she had given herself, had prepared her for such an onslaught of emotion. She kept telling herself that she had resisted him, that she had held on to her pride, but she couldn't circumnavigate the crux of the matter, which was, like it or not, she had wanted him.

When she had broken off her relationship with Michael, she had known, unerringly, that she was not about to make involvement with a man top of her list of priorities. Not for a very long time, at which point whoever took his place would be different from him but basically a kind, thoughtful and similarly undemanding person. She realised now that it had never occurred to her, even in her wildest dreams, that she would be attracted to a man who was so supremely different from him in every respect that it knocked the breath out of her. She wondered whether that indicated that whatever she felt for Antonio Silver was at the very worst no more than a bad case of physical desire. It frightened her because she had never felt that for anyone in her life before. In fact, she had never considered herself capable of feeling it. But, she decided, physical desire was little more than a temporary inconvenience. She would get over it in no time at all. Life could carry on as normal. That watery surface which had been violently stirred would eventually subside back into its usual ripple-free, glassy condition. That was what she wanted, wasn't it?

For the first time in ages, she slept through her alarm clock and was awakened by Benjamin thumping on her door.

She struggled out of bed and met his concerned gaze with a twinge of guilt.

'Are you all right, my dear?' he asked solicitously, and she nodded.

'I don't know what happened,' she confessed, rubbing her eyes with her thumbs and stifling a yawn. 'I didn't fall asleep for ages last night.'

'Must have had something on your mind,' he said conversationally. 'I hope you haven't forgotten that today is library day.'

'Give me five minutes.'

'You're a woman. I'll give you an hour.'

She was ready in considerably less time than that, dressed in a smart pleated cream skirt with a cream blouse neatly tucked in and her hair carefully coiled at the back of her neck.

'You look as though you should be teaching Sunday school in that outfit,' Benjamin remarked with his usual candour.

'How nice to be greeted with such flattery,' Corinna said wryly. He had already eaten his breakfast, and she quickly gulped down a cup of coffee. There was no sign of Antonio anywhere, not that she expected to see him around. It was nine-thirty. He would be out and about, hopefully until well into the night. She was going to make quite sure that she retired to bed, or at least to some other, very obscure part of the house, well before he was likely to make an entrance. If she kept that up, she thought, for a few days at any rate, she would feel more equipped to face him with the necessary self-control.

As luck would have it, he was not safely ensconced in some other part of the county, but lounging indolently at the foot of the staircase, sifting through the post on the small table in the hall. He had one hand in his pocket, and the lines of his muscular body, half turned away from them, were elegant and graceful. Corinna's eyes flicked to him and she had to force herself to smile as he turned to face them.

Benjamin's hand was resting lightly on her arm, and the silver-grey eyes glittered at that, then lifted to look at her with a sardonic question.

He was dressed in green cords and a pale green and tan shirt, and he didn't, she thought, look anything like a man on the verge of leaving the house for business. That didn't matter, though, since she wasn't going to be around. She said in a high, bright voice, 'Good morning. Lovely day outside.'

He didn't answer. 'Where are you going?' The question was directed at Benjamin, who bristled for a while, partly out of habit, then informed his son that they were off to the library.

'Surely not both of you?'

'As a matter of fact, we are,' Corinna said, riled. 'Both of us.'

'Why?' Benjamin asked.

Antonio surveyed them both, then he smiled coolly. 'Because I need the services of your——' he paused, then said '—nursemaid. You type, don't you?'

Corinna met his eyes with dislike. 'In a manner of speaking. If you want a secretary, though, then I suggest you get in touch with an agency. I doubt I'm anywhere near the standard you'd expect.'

'And I doubt you have any idea of the standard I would expect.' He reverted his attention to his father. 'Would you feel able to go on your own?' And Benjamin, Corinna was horrified to see, nodded. Bye-bye, hostility, hello, Mr Amicable. She couldn't believe it.

'Good. Meet me in the library.' He walked off and Corinna helplessly watched as Benjamin left, then she stormed along to the library, her hands on her hips.

Antonio was waiting for her, sitting at the desk with the computer terminal switched on.

'What,' she all but yelled, 'is the meaning of this?'

He turned to face her. 'You shouldn't use that tone of voice,' he drawled lazily, 'you sound like a school-teacher, and not a very pleasant one at that.'

'I don't feel very pleasant!' Her face was red. 'I don't work for you! How dare you act as though you can just— just commandeer my services!' She was spluttering and getting angrier by the minute at the cool little smile on his face.

'Strong words,' he said mildly. 'Pull a chair and sit down, I'll show you what I want you to do.'

He turned his back on her and began fiddling with the keyboard, and Corinna stared at his profile with loathing.

'I can't type,' she informed him bluntly, dragging a chair alongside him.

'Of course you can. More talents for which you've been praised to the high heavens by my father. He told me that you taught yourself the rudiments and then practised until now you're quite acceptable. So——' he faced her and she felt her pulse rate begin to rise '—no modesty, please. Here's what I want you to do.'

'*Here's what you want me to do*? You see fit to slot me into place as temporary secretary, and you don't even have the manners to say *please*?'

He shot her an expression of such mock horror that she was tempted to sock him on the jaw. 'A thousand apologies. *Please*. Is that better?' He didn't wait for her answer. He proceeded to flick through a file of letters, briefly informing her what he wanted done, showing her the basics of the computer, then when he was finished, he said, 'Any questions?'

'Yes.'

'What?' He clasped his hands behind his head and surveyed her.

'When are you going to be leaving?'

That made him laugh, then he raked his fingers through his hair and shook his head. 'Who knows?' His eyes narrowed. 'When the time is right.'

They swopped chairs and she began the typing. His letters were very like him. To the point, leaving the reader in no doubt as to who was dealing the cards.

It was two and a half hours later by the time she completed the lot with, she had to admit to herself, relatively little fuss.

'I'm finished,' she said to him, walking into the lounge where he was surrounded by documents and several brochures on various aspects of the pharmaceutical business.

She handed him the sheaf of letters without any pleasantries and he flicked through them, nodding, then he put them on the table and said smoothly, 'Now wasn't that more fun than trekking around a library with my father?'

'Oh,' she said sarcastically, 'it was heaps of fun. I've never had such a fun-filled morning in my entire life. Please feel free to hurl all your correspondence at me. In fact, better still, I could just set up camp by the computer terminal so that I'm always at the ready.'

He grinned, showing white, even teeth, and another flash of that devastating charm.

'What a kind offer,' he said, raising his eyebrows sardonically. 'Sit down and have something to drink.'

'I'd rather not.'

'Suit yourself. I shouldn't get too overheated by the little job you've just done though, because——' he paused for effect '—I'll be using your services again. Less time for you to spend making eyes at my father. Not that you do that, dear me, no, but just in case, better safe than sorry, don't you agree?'

'You——!'

'Bastard?'

'Yes!' she yelled and he grinned back at her, not at all put out by her rage.

'This may be a cliché, but has anyone ever told you that you're beautiful when you're angry?'

The soft chuckle followed her to the door, which she slammed behind her, and then continued in her head for the remainder of the day.

Not even the fact that he had disappeared some time towards the middle of the afternoon could dull the teeth-grinding anger she felt at his high-handed behaviour.

Benjamin was exhausted by his trip, and retired to bed at seven with his library books—all of them computer books, what else?—and she settled down for an evening of simmering in her own company.

She was in the middle of helping herself to some of Edna's pot roast when she heard someone at the door, and she felt her body stiffen in anticipation of facing Antonio. Where the hell was his key? she asked herself, more than ready for a fight, as she half ran to open the door. What was the point of having a key if you continued to drag people away from their meals to open doors for you? Typical. He probably wouldn't even apologise for the inconvenience.

She was in the grip of a good, healthy anger, when she pulled the door open, but it wasn't Antonio standing in front of her. It was a woman, *the* woman. Corinna knew that instantly because the brunette standing in front of her just matched the voice down the telephone. They stared at each other, then Corinna said politely, 'May I help you?'

'I doubt that,' the woman said, 'but Antonio might. Is he available?' The same perfect English, with the overtones of an accent, that had smokily let slip just how well she was acquainted with him the evening before on the telephone.

She was small, small enough to make Corinna feel like a giant, with very short dark hair and black eyes. Her skin was flawless and tanned, and in her tan dress, belted tightly at the waist, she looked expensive. Expensive and hard, like a beautiful, priceless stone.

She was smiling back at Corinna but her eyes were cold and assessing.

'Do you work here?' she asked with a hint of impatience. 'I would like to enter.'

'Of course.' Corinna stepped aside and the woman said to her, with a little flick of her head, 'My bags are in the taxi. If you wouldn't mind...?'

Three cases, to be exact. The taxi driver was bringing them to the doorstep, very subservient, so Corinna assumed that the tip must have been enormous, because from her limited experience of taxi drivers they rarely gave you the time of day.

The dark-haired woman was looking around her, but without any real interest, and as soon as Corinna had closed the front door, she said with the same cold smile, 'Perhaps you could tell Antonio that Maria Felucci is here.'

'Perhaps I couldn't,' Corinna said, looking down at the woman. 'He's not home.'

'Oh.' She didn't like that. The black brows met in a frown and the polite smile was discarded.

Was this his lover? Corinna wondered with a sour taste of jealousy in her mouth. It didn't surprise her. Maria Felucci was beautiful, with the sort of sultry, sexy dark looks that not even her severely cut dress could camouflage. She had an hourglass figure, all curves and small-waisted, and her beautifully manicured hands were tipped with long fingernails that had been painted burgundy to match her belt. She looked as though she had never stepped into a pair of jeans in her entire life and probably slummed around her house in little Armani numbers.

'And can you tell me when he is expected back?'

'I'm afraid I can't,' Corinna said. 'He returns home at unpredictable hours.'

'Home?' Maria's eyebrows rose into cynical arches. 'This is not Antonio's *home*. His *home* is in Italy.'

Corinna smiled politely and wished that she hadn't bothered to open the door.

'Well, show me to the living area, then. Somewhere where I may wait for him.'

'Follow me, please.' She walked towards the lounge, wondering how long Antonio's charming companion planned on staying. From the looks of those bags, several months, but then she probably, Corinna thought acidly, didn't believe in travelling light, even for overnight stops.

'Can I get you something to drink?' Corinna asked, and Maria said coolly, 'I spoke to you on the telephone last night, is that right? Are you one of the maids?'

'I work for Mr Silver, Antonio's father. I'm his private nurse.'

The dark eyes glanced over her speculatively.

'I'm sure.' She allowed a little pause, then said, as though the subject of Corinna, her place in the household, her very presence, had ceased to be of any interest whatsoever, 'No, you cannot get me anything. I shall sit here until Antonio returns.' She had carried a Louis Vuitton briefcase with her into the lounge and she patted it. 'I have some papers to go through. That will keep me occupied, and Antonio will not be long, I think. I told him that I would be coming.'

She snapped open the briefcase, extracted several papers and didn't bother to glance in Corinna's direction as she let herself out of the lounge and stormed off back to the kitchen.

So Antonio had invited her, had he? How cosy. How intimate. She was surprised that the woman hadn't asked to be shown up to his bedroom to wait for him until he returned.

Her food, of course, had gone stone cold and she threw it away, quickly washed her plate and then made herself a cup of coffee. She had planned on an early night, but now she found that she wanted to remain up until Antonio came back. He would head immediately to the kitchen. Like everyone else in the household he had unconsciously fallen in with them in treating it as the main hub of the house, and Corinna waited there for another forty-five minutes, until she heard his footsteps outside.

He wasn't expecting her. He stopped in the doorway, his grey eyes narrowing, then he walked in, taking off his jacket to deposit it on the back of one of the kitchen chairs and loosening his tie.

'You look,' he drawled, with his back to her as he helped himself to a piece of Stilton from the fridge and a glass of wine, 'as though you've lost five pounds and not only have you found nothing, you've also discovered that you haven't got enough money for the last bus home.'

'Very humorous,' Corinna said coldly.

'I suppose you're going to lecture me on my arrogant behaviour in getting you to type a few little letters for me.' He gave her a quick, stripping glance before he took a seat opposite her. There was hot food in the oven, but he chose to eat slices of Edna's home-made bread and more of the Stilton from the fridge.

'No, I was not,' Corinna said, her hackles rising.

'Oh, good. I've had a tiring afternoon and I'm in no mood to sit through a sermon.'

He looked tired and she resisted the urge to sympathise. The man didn't deserve sympathy in any shape or form.

'Poor you,' she said. 'What a cruel world it is.'

He grinned and some of the tiredness left his face. 'You are quite a pick-me-up sometimes, do you know that?'

That made her blush and fidget. Throwaway remarks like that disconcerted her, made her forget how much she basically disliked him.

He stood up and she expected him to return to the fridge to pour himself a top-up of wine, but he didn't. He came behind her and leaned over her, with his hands resting on the back of her chair, his face so close to hers that she could feel his warm breath on her neck.

'So what's on your mind, then? You might as well get it out of your system before you go up in smoke.'

She found that she couldn't move a muscle, never mind respond to his calculated sarcasm.

'That,' he murmured, 'wouldn't do at all.'

He straightened and moved back to his chair, having poured himself a long glass of mineral water.

Without him looming behind her, swamping her with his presence, she finally managed to find her voice, and she said with a tight smile, 'Thank you for your concern,' crossly aware that he was grinning again. 'And you're quite wrong. I haven't got anything *to get out of my system*. In fact, it's only by chance that you found me here.' She lowered her eyes at that untruth. 'But while I *am* here, you might like to know that your girlfriend is waiting for you in the lounge.'

There was a swift intake of breath, then he muttered an oath which she didn't manage to catch.

'When did she arrive?'

So he wasn't denying that Maria Felucci of the impeccable grooming was his girlfriend. She hadn't expected him to but, for some reason, that still hurt. No one likes to be played with, she thought, and this was final proof that all his flirting, which had left her so hot and bothered, was little more than a game to him.

'At least an hour ago,' Corinna said. 'Shouldn't you be rushing to her side? She's probably at the end of her tether in there, even if she did say that she had a lot of paperwork to go through.'

He stood up with a preoccupied frown.

'I wonder what Maria's doing here,' he said, still frowning, and Corinna smiled sweetly.

'Do you? I was told that you were expecting her.'

'I suppose I should have been,' Antonio said, but he didn't enlarge on that statement. 'Has she made herself at home?' he asked, running his fingers through his hair.

Corinna had no idea what to make of that question. In fact she was puzzled at his reaction to his girlfriend's arrival, especially since he had asked her to come.

'Oh, yes,' she said, not dwelling on that. 'Quite at home. I offered her food and drink, made sure that her suitcases were neatly stacked in the corner of the hall.

Nothing was too much, considering that I'm little more than a maid.'

He laughed and looked at her from under his thick, black lashes. 'I can imagine,' he murmured, heading for the door.

After he had gone, Corinna remained where she was and made herself a cup of tea. Why should she scurry off to bed just because Antonio's girlfriend was on the scene? She was not going to let that affect her behaviour in the slightest. So she made herself take her time over her tea, and she made herself stay put even when she heard voices in the hall, then the sound of approaching footsteps.

True, her fingers curled around the teacup and she had to make a conscious effort to relax them, but she didn't stand up with a view to pretending that she was just on her way to bed. Why the hell should she?

Antonio pushed open the kitchen door and Maria walked past him, her exquisite, cat-like face still wearing the remnants of the smile from whatever intimate joke they had just been sharing.

As soon as her eyes fell on Corinna, the smile died and the hard glitter which had been there earlier, when she had first arrived, was back in the black eyes.

An aeroplane ride, Corinna thought, a bumpy journey in a taxi, an hour's wait in the lounge, and still Maria managed to look as though she had just stepped out of a beauty parlour. Corinna wished that she was wearing something slightly more presentable than the skirt and blouse which made her feel incredibly frumpy in comparison.

'We meet again,' Maria said, resting her hand lightly but significantly on Antonio's arm. 'How nice.' Her eyes definitely did not agree with that sentiment, however. 'You should have joined me in the lounge. We could

## NO COST! NO OBLIGATION TO BUY!
## NO PURCHASE NECESSARY!

## PLAY "LUCKY 7"
## AND GET AS MANY AS SIX FREE GIFTS...

# HOW TO PLAY:

**1** With a coin, carefully scratch away the silver panel opposite. You will now be eligible to receive two or more FREE books, and possibly other gifts, depending on what is revealed beneath the scratch off area.

**2** When you return this card, you'll receive specially selected **Mills & Boon romances**. We'll send you the books and gifts you qualify for absolutely FREE, and at the same time we'll reserve you a subscription to our Reader Service.

**3** If we don't hear from you, within 10 days we'll send you six brand new romances to read and enjoy every month for just £1.90 each, the same price as the books in the shops. There is no extra charge for postage and handling. There are no hidden extras.

**4** When you join the Mills & Boon Reader Service, you'll also get our FREE monthly Newsletter, featuring author news, horoscopes, penfriends, competitions.

**5** You are under no obligation, and may cancel or suspend your subscription at any time simply by writing to us.

**You'll love your cuddly teddy. His brown eyes and cute face are sure to make you smile.**

# Play "Lucky 7"

Just scratch away the silver panel with a coin.
Then check below to see which gifts you get.

**YES!** I have scratched away the silver panel. Please send me all the gifts for which I qualify. I understand that I am under no obligation to purchase any books, as explained on the opposite page. I am over 18 years of age.

MS/MRS/MISS/MR                                                                                11A4R
_____

ADDRESS
_____

_____

POSTCODE                          SIGNATURE

 **WORTH FOUR FREE BOOKS**
**PLUS A CUDDLY TEDDY AND MYSTERY GIFT**

 **WORTH FOUR FREE BOOKS**
**PLUS A MYSTERY GIFT**

 **WORTH FOUR FREE BOOKS**

  **WORTH TWO FREE BOOKS**

## MILLS & BOON 'NO RISK' GUARANTEE

- You're not required to buy a single book!
- You must be completely satisfied or you may cancel at any time simply by writing to us. You will receive no more books; you'll have no further obligation.
- The free books and gifts you receive from this offer remain yours to keep no matter what you decide.

**Mills & Boon Reader Service**
**FREEPOST**
**P.O. Box 236**
**Croydon**
**Surrey**
**CR9 9EL**

NO
STAMP
NEEDED

have chatted, so much more interesting than boring papers, no?'

She said something in rapid Italian to Antonio, who laughed, and then said, 'We mustn't speak Italian whilst you're over here.'

'Or at least,' Maria amended with a sultry little laugh, 'not while we're in public.'

'Oh, please,' Corinna said, forcing a smile which made the muscles in her jaw ache, 'go right ahead.' I really have no interest in what you two are saying, her voice implied, and Antonio raised his eyebrows, interpreting the hidden message behind her words.

'I was just on my way out, actually,' she added.

Antonio looked as though he didn't quite believe that. 'Were you?' He eyed her almost full cup of tea. 'Why don't you stay and finish your cup of tea with us?'

'Yes, do,' Maria said coldly. She sat down at the kitchen table and those amazing, oddly hard black eyes focused on Corinna's face. 'You mustn't leave because of us. We shall have enough time on our own, shall we not, Antonio darling?'

Antonio didn't answer. He moved off towards the fridge, ignoring Maria's little patting actions for him to sit next to her, and extracted a half-bottle of wine and two glasses.

'Will you join us or are you going to stay with your tea?'

Wearing the same smile, which now seemed to be painfully plastered to her face, Corinna shook her head and said, 'I'll stick to tea.'

'I thought so.'

Maria was listening to this brief interchange with clear disapproval. 'You don't drink?' she asked with a little laugh. 'How noble, darling. I myself adore wine, and I adore champagne even more. It's all I ever drink at home, isn't it, Antonio?'

'Really?' Corinna said politely, refusing the temptation to ask whether dehydration wasn't a problem with her. She was feeling more uncomfortable by the minute and she gulped down a mouthful of tea, making sure not to watch as Antonio sat down next to Maria and once again the smooth, possessive hand stroked his arm.

It was impossible to glean from his expression what he was thinking, but then she had seen enough of him to realise that he was a master of self-control. He was also not the type, she felt instinctively, to indulge in public displays of emotion.

'So,' Maria said, breaking the silence, 'I understand you have been working here for quite some while. A nurse, are you not? And you don't find it a little——' she made a little move as she tried to think of the right word '—dull?'

'That's what Antonio asked me when he first arrived,' Corinna said, taking another swig of tea and gratefully noticing that the cup would soon be empty enough to warrant a departure, 'and the answer is no. I don't find it dull at all. I enjoy it, or else I'd leave.'

Maria said something in Italian once again and then pouted prettily. 'Oh, I forgot. Must not speak in Italian.'

'No, you mustn't,' Antonio said with a hint of impatience.

'I was just saying that I can understand Antonio asking you that. He, as myself, moves in very aggressive circles.'

'And what do you do?' Corinna asked, because the statement demanded the question.

'I run my parents' pharmaceutical company,' Maria said. 'It is small, but successful, and it takes quite a bit of work.'

'I'm sure.' Corinna stood up. 'Well, I really must get to bed now.' With a slight trace of alarm, she saw that Antonio had stood up as well. He had placed his hand on Maria's shoulder and she covered it with her own.

What a gorgeous couple, Corinna thought sourly. Both dark, both good-looking, and just there, with her hand over his, begging for a photographer to come along and take their picture.

'Maria will be staying the night,' he said, looking down at the sleek dark head, its sexy face upturned to his. 'Where can she sleep?'

'Oh, darling! Is that really a problem? I'm sure your bedroom could accommodate little me.'

'I'm sure it could,' he murmured, and that brought a smile of feline pleasure to the full red mouth.

'You stay here, finish your drink,' he told Maria, not looking at her. 'I'll take your bags up to the room. I'll be down in a few minutes.'

He didn't give her the opportunity to protest at that. He ushered Corinna out, shutting the kitchen door behind them with a soft click. As soon as they were out in the hall, she turned to him and said, 'I don't think that Benjamin is going to be thrilled with this.'

'Since when are you my father's voice?'

She turned away at that and he caught her arm, pulling her to face him. 'What is the problem here?'

'Problem?' She gave him her best wide-eyed innocent look. 'What problem?'

He sighed impatiently and released her. 'Look, I know my father won't be too impressed by Maria's sudden arrival here. She tends to——' he searched for the right words '—do things on impulse.'

'There's no need to explain anything to me.'

'There is when you're standing there looking at me as though I've just returned home from looting and

pillaging.' They stared at each other, and her skin began
to prickle. He had a very intense, relentless stare.

'You don't like her, do you?'

Corinna shrugged and looked down. 'I don't know
the woman.'

'How diplomatic.'

It comes from years of nursing, she wanted to say,
and also, she admitted truthfully, from the fact that I
don't want you to think that I give a damn what you
do. Which, she told herself, I don't.

'Oh, go to hell.' She began walking off and he pulled
her back by her arm, twisting her to face him.

'I don't like people walking off when I'm talking to
them,' he said in a hard voice, and she glared back at
him.

'Tough. You're not my boss.'

'Maybe you're a little jealous? Is that it? Did you think
that some harmless flirting entitles you to a few rights
of ownership?'

Corinna looked at him incredulously.

'Rights of ownership?' she asked, laughing, she
thought, a little hysterically. 'Don't be absurd.'

He frowned darkly. 'Absurd?'

'Yes. Absurd.' The word rolled off her tongue easily.
'Absurd,' she repeated. 'If you really must know, I'm
far too sensible to have my head turned by a little
harmless flirting!'

She looked into his dark handsome face and felt a
flicker of panic, thinking that he would see through her
pretence of casualness. She had never been casual when
it came to her emotions, she couldn't conceive of flirting
with the gay ease which some women possessed. Her
mother had been a terrific flirt, but that didn't stop her
from lecturing her daughter on the dangers of carrying
on with men, as she called it. Corinna had taken that

advice with a pinch of salt, but something must have stuck because she had never cultivated the talent.

'I never thought I'd meet a woman who would say that to me,' he murmured, his eyes glinting with amusement, and she offered him a smile in return.

'No? Well, perhaps I just haven't met anyone worth flirting with.'

He hadn't expected that. His face darkened, and he looked as though he was going to pursue the conversation, but they were both aware of Maria's presence behind the kitchen door and, while he was hesitating, Corinna walked off towards her bedroom, taking the stairs two at a time, not looking back to see whether he had returned to the kitchen, or else was behind her with the cases.

She wished that she could hold the little flare of triumph at her parting shot, take it to bed with her, but already it was fading, replaced by something sickening and sharp. The savage claws of jealousy.

# CHAPTER SIX

BENJAMIN was not a happy man. Corinna went to his bedroom the following morning to find that Antonio had already been there and had explained about Maria's arrival. He had yet to meet her but for some reason he had already decided that he didn't like her.

'What kind of manners do you call that?' he stormed to Corinna as she bustled around the room, checking his supply of tablets, picking up computer manuals from the ground and stacking them neatly on the bedside table.

'Well?' he asked aggressively. 'Is that the Mediterranean temperament just to fly over to a stranger's house for an indefinite stay, *without even having been invited*? Well, is it?'

Corinna mentioned, non-committally, that she had known quite a few Italians in her time and no, she didn't think that that was a national trait.

'Stop fussing!' he ordered her. 'And why have you gone back to wearing those dull clothes? I preferred you in that pinky affair you wore the other day.'

The sudden change of topic didn't surprise her in the slightest. Benjamin had a mind that tended to whirl off in odd directions occasionally and she had learnt to take it in her stride.

'It's going to be cold and miserable today,' she said calmly. 'I thought I'd wear something warm and comfortable.' What she didn't say was that she felt safer dressed like this. Safe, impersonal, capable of functioning in the efficient, detached manner which had been her lifelong companion. Her clothes, right now, were a barrier against that other disturbing side that she felt in Antonio's presence.

'Pah!' he barked, surveying her off-white jumper and sober grey skirt with distaste. 'Now that I'm back on my feet, so to speak, you and I are going to take a little trip into London and I'm going to get you a really splendid outfit.'

Corinna looked at him, appalled. This was the first time he had ever suggested anything of the sort. In fact, it was the first time that he had ever really made an issue out of her clothing.

'Please don't do that,' she said hastily.

'Then for God's sake don't wear such drab clothes.' He looked at her from under his brows, then he said gruffly, 'You're much too pretty to hide away behind those bland colours. Anyway, what's she like?'

'I hardly spoke to her at all,' she murmured. 'She seems—interesting.'

'Rude, that's what she seems to me. Rude, rude, rude.'

'She *was* invited.'

His eyebrows shot up at that one. 'Says who? Not Antonio.'

'Well, whatever.' Corinna shrugged and Benjamin eyed her irritably. 'Is that all the reaction I can expect from you? What does she look like, then? You can at least tell me that.'

'You'll see for yourself in due course,' Corinna answered, opening the bedroom door, and he glared at her.

'Attractive, I suppose?' he asked, coming close to her and holding her arm. 'I don't know what she is to my son, but if she's—if they're—well, let's just say that I don't see him going out with anyone who wasn't reasonably attractive.'

'She's attractive.' Corinna didn't want to talk about her. She foresaw some very uncomfortable encounters with Maria, if that spark of hostility in her eyes was anything to go by, and the thought of that wasn't comforting. Maria, she thought, was what her mother would describe as a man's woman: the sort of woman who only really blossomed in the company of men, and was usually downright antagonistic towards members of her own sex.

She was nowhere to be seen as they entered the kitchen, and they were informed by Edna, who had briefly spoken to Antonio before he left the house, that Maria was not a morning person, at least not unless work called.

This little piece of insight was communicated in a voice dripping with disapproval and Benjamin looked as though that was just what he had expected. Corinna almost felt sorry for the absent Maria, then she thought of those hard, disdainful black eyes and decided that she would save her sympathy for a worthier cause.

She drank her coffee, chatting to Benjamin about this and that while he ate his usual hearty breakfast, but when she asked him how he would like to spend the day, he surprised her by saying that she could have the day off.

'Take yourself up to London,' he suggested. 'I won't be back until late afternoon. I want to visit a few bookshops and Antonio's arranged for me to have lunch with him, and one of his colleagues who will be working at the subsidiary over here. In fact——' he began buttering another slice of toast with lowered eyes '—the gentleman will be joining us for supper, so perhaps you could make sure that you're back by six-thirty?'

'We're having company for dinner?' Corinna asked, surprised, and he said in a lofty voice, 'Stranger things *have* been known to happen.'

'Not in a long time though, if you don't mind my saying,' Edna interjected, and Benjamin snapped testily, 'As a matter of fact, I do mind. Just you make sure that you do me proud on the food front.'

'And when have you ever had cause to complain about my cooking?' She wiped her hands on her apron and turned to face him, and Benjamin threw her an alarmed look.

'Not recently,' he conceded. 'But there's always a first.' He stood up, patted Corinna on the shoulder, and then gave her a kiss on her cheek, which made her go red.

As soon as he was out of the room, Edna shook her head and said, 'He's going mad, he is. One minute he won't leave the house for love nor money, the next minute wild horses can't keep him out of that car. Crazy as a coot.'

Corinna laughed, but later, as she strolled through Covent Garden, feeling sorry for the tourists who hurried past her with the anxious expressions of people half frozen on what should have been a warm summer day, she had to admit that Benjamin's behaviour had been a bit odd. First all that ado over her clothes, then vanishing for a day's outing without so much as a quiver of apprehension. The trip to the library must have boosted his confidence no end. Or maybe Antonio had awakened another side to him, just as, she thought uneasily, he had done to her.

She arrived back at the house at precisely six-thirty. It had been a lazy, enjoyable day off. She had met one of her friends for lunch, strolled and window-shopped, read her book on the train back, and she was feeling quite refreshed.

She made her way up to her bedroom, opened the door and then stopped. There was a dress on her bed. Not just any dress. An exquisite dress in midnight blue, with a deep-cut neckline and a slim, fitted waist. And it was expensive. Corinna was not *au fait* with fashion but she recognised the label immediately.

'Like it?' Benjamin asked from behind her, and she turned to face him, ready to inform him, kindly of course, that she couldn't possibly accept it, when she stopped at the eager, hesitant expression on his face.

She smiled at him. 'What am I going to do with you?' she chided. 'Is this how you've been spending your day?'

'Just thought you might like a little something to wear tonight,' he said, his lined face going red. 'Got your size from sneaking a look at one of your dresses in the cupboard. Hope you don't mind, my dear.'

'Mind?' She approached him and gave him a hug. 'It's beautiful and I shall enjoy wearing it.' At which sentiment he looked thrilled, clearing his throat and patting her arm.

'Our guest is expected at seven-thirty. Drinks in the lounge.' He turned to go, then spun back round to face her. 'Almost forgot.' He held out a beautiful diamond necklace. 'Was my mother's, you know. Hasn't been worn for a very long time. Antonio's mother didn't care for it. I'd like you to have it.'

Corinna looked at the necklace, stunned into speechlessness. Finally, she said in a small voice that she couldn't possibly, but he was already putting it into her hands and she stared down at it.

'Please,' he murmured. 'It would make an old man very happy.' At which she sighed and accepted it.

'But only for tonight,' she said, 'then you must have it back. It belongs around the neck of your son's future wife.'

'Agreed,' Benjamin said with a disarming smile, and he was gone, leaving her to get dressed.

She took her time, lingering in the hot bath, then unhurriedly applying her make-up. She wanted to save the dress for last. She didn't think that she had ever owned anything quite so beautiful. On her sixteenth birthday her mother, in a surprisingly unexpected gesture, had treated her to a lovely dress, but it had been nothing like this. This was sexy and that dress, all those years ago, had been innocent. Her mother was still, even at Corinna's age, finding it difficult to believe that her daughter was growing up. The dress, Corinna had realised much later, had been a subconscious attempt to keep her in the little-girl role which was easier to handle.

And Michael had never once given her anything to do with her sexuality. He had bought her perfume in the past, and books, twice he had given her jumpers; but this—this was spectacular.

When she slipped it on, she stood looking at her reflection in the mirror with a mixture of amazement and breathless excitement. She had left her hair loose and it flowed down her back like rich cornsilk. Not bad, she told the reflection with a grin. She twirled, looked into the mirror over her shoulder, and then laughed self-consciously at the gesture of pure vanity. She was not vain by nature, and anyway, working impossibly long shifts at the hospital, devoting all her time and energies to patients, had never left her the time to be vain. It was odd and a little frightening to see the glitter in her eyes as she looked at herself now. There were a lot of things, she was discovering, a lot of traits which had been lying dormant, waiting to awaken, and now they had. The lid of Pandora's box had been opened and much had been lost forever.

She was the last to arrive. She could hear the low murmur of voices as she approached the lounge and she took a deep breath as she pushed open the door, instinctively turning to the one certain, friendly face in the room, Benjamin's. His eyes lit up as soon as he saw her and he gave her an approving nod.

'Doesn't she look radiant?' he asked no one in particular, and one of the guests, a dark-haired man in his early thirties, said warmly, 'Beautiful.'

Antonio didn't say anything, but out of the corner of her eye she knew that he was staring at her, his grey eyes narrowed and watchful.

Then the conversation resumed. Benjamin was talking to the guest and he called her over to introduce her.

Corinna felt as though she were floating on air. Roberto kissed her hand and when he looked at her his dark eyes were warm, as warm as the smile on his face. There was another couple there, English, friends of Benjamin's, whom she later learnt he had invited on the spur of the moment.

Corinna was introduced to them as well. I'll pretend that Antonio isn't here, she thought, but she knew that that was impossible because his very presence was responsible for the fluttering in her stomach. He strolled up behind her and said coldly in her ear, 'Can I get you a drink?'

She turned around, and his eyes flicked over her, then returned to her face. 'Stunning,' he said. Behind him, she could see Maria's black, glittering eyes looking at her with dislike. She was sitting on a chair by the fireside, a glass of wine in her hand and, even seated, Corinna could see that her dress was a minuscule black number exposing quite a bit of thigh and cleavage.

He raised one finger, which brushed against her neck, sending little volts of electricity running through her, and toyed with the necklace, then he let his hand drop.

'I see that you're not too full of moral rectitude to accept little gifts from my father? This necklace is worth a small fortune. Did you suggest it or did he?'

Corinna gritted her teeth together and tried to stay calm. 'I didn't even know of its existence until——'

'Until he thrust it into your hands? Perhaps holding a gun to your head so that you couldn't refuse?'

'I did refuse. People are looking at us.'

'I have never cared what people thought,' he said grimly, 'and I certainly don't intend to start now. And the dress? Another gift?'

She flushed uncomfortably.

'Ah, no need to answer that one. It's written all over your face.' He poured her a glass of white wine, his movements controlled. 'Are you going to try and tell me that you also tried, desperately, to refuse that little gift as well?' His voice was low and harsh, and his eyes were dangerously cold.

'I'm not going to try and tell you anything, since you don't want to hear.'

His mouth thinned and for the first time she saw the dull red of anger on his face. He adjusted his body so that his back was towards the assembled guests, and she was forced to look up at him because he was blocking her vision of everything else. He was dressed formally, in a dark suit, with a white shirt, though the prerequisite tie was absent, and the raw animal magnetism was evident in the way the cut of the suit cleaved to his body. She slid her eyes a little to one side to avoid the sheer knock-out power of the man.

'Don't push me,' he grated.

'Then don't push *me*!' she hissed by way of response, not allowing her awareness of him to get in the way of her anger. 'I have no intention of keeping this necklace, and as for the dress, well, you can have it if you like, as soon as I step out of it, if it means so much to you that I accept nothing from your father, however kind his intentions might be!'

Their eyes clashed and she saw a thread of uncertainty flicker on his face, although he was still frowning.

'I'd love some more white wine,' she heard herself say, buoyed by her own refusal to be reduced to stammering incoherence by the sheer force of his personality.

He turned to pour her some and Corinna saw in the background that Maria was beginning to look a little impatient. Constance, Benjamin's friend, was chatting to her, but the conversation was not capturing her attention nearly as much as Antonio and Corinna. She couldn't take her eyes off them.

Corinna gave her a little wave which was met with a nod of recognition, then the black eyes moved away from her and back to Constance.

'I think Maria wants you to join her,' Corinna said politely to Antonio.

'So?'

'Silly me,' she replied sarcastically, 'of course that's no reason for you to do anything of the sort. Why should you? You do as you please, don't you? Just as you feel free to say what you want. Anyway, she'll probably wait for you until the cows come home.'

His grey eyes were lit with grudging admiration as he looked at her, which changed suddenly to mocking amusement. 'And you disapprove?' he asked softly.

She forced herself to look at that hard, handsome face, her body instantly on edge at the change in his voice. 'I don't *disapprove*,' she said politely, 'I just think that any woman who's prepared to wait for any man must be a little mad.'

'And I think that any woman who's prepared to bury herself in the middle of nowhere because she's scared of life is a little mad as well.'

Her head snapped up. 'I am *not* scared of life!'

'My father has extremely good taste if he picked your dress out for you,' he said by way of response. 'For the first time you look like a woman who's proud of the way she looks, instead of someone hiding behind a uniform of dull clothes.' His eyes roamed over her at leisure, which made her even angrier.

'Thank you for that valuable little observation,' she bit out. 'I'll cherish it in the years to come.'

He smiled again, amused. Triumphs scored against Antonio Silver were always short-lived, weren't they? He always managed to swerve the conversation right back to where he wanted it, didn't he? He was still looking at her, prepared, no doubt, to antagonise her a little bit more before he rejoined his now highly impatient girlfriend, but he didn't get the chance. Thankfully.

They were joined by Benjamin and his long-time friend Austin, who it transpired was Antonio's godfather, and that was the last time that Corinna was alone with Antonio, which suited her fine.

She sat next to Constance at the dinner-table, with Roberto on her left, and after three glasses of wine she hardly noticed Maria's malicious darting glances.

Roberto, it turned out, was a charmer. His English was not as good as either Maria's or Antonio's, and he spent the evening trying to persuade her that a little personal tutoring from her wouldn't go amiss.

With uncustomary reckless abandon, Corinna found that she was in the perfect frame of mind to be persuaded into flirting. When, between starters and the main course, he held her hand, to see whether it was as soft and graceful as it looked, she smiled with delight, vaguely aware of Antonio's grey eyes flitting across to her, and the hard set of his mouth.

As they enjoyed the main course, a splendid affair of pork with cherries and an assortment of vegetables, which Edna brought to the table with something resembling a smirk on her face, Roberto's low murmur succeeded in eliminating the rest of the party, without succumbing to rudeness, so that she felt as if she were the sole object of his attentions. It was lovely. It was fun, and if she was getting black looks from Antonio from across the table, then that gave her a certain wicked pleasure as well.

'I feel as eef I know you all my life,' he whispered expressively into her ear. 'How ees thees possible? Eef only——' he cast her a woeful look and she grinned at the theatricality of it '—I speak the Ingleesh better, no?' He spoke rather more loudly than he had intended into a brief lull in the conversation, but by this time Corinna felt altogether too light-hearted to be bothered by that. 'How am I to get through with thees bad Ingleesh?' he asked, lowering his voice and rolling his eyes upwards, and Corinna laughed gaily. She felt wonderful. Light-headed, full of fun, without a care in the world.

'Maybe,' Antonio drawled from across the table, 'you weren't the right choice for the job, Roberto.' There was an uncomfortable silence while everyone tried to work out whether that was meant as a joke or not. His voice had been distinctly lacking in humour. 'Maybe,' he continued, 'I should get someone whose Ingleesh is a little more accomplished.' He ate a mouthful of Edna's superb bread and butter pudding, and after another long, awkward silence, Benjamin said something, and conversation resumed. Across the table, Antonio caught Corinna's eye and she glared at him. Poor Roberto.

'I'm sure he didn't mean that, Roberto,' she said softly, smiling at him, and he shook his head.

'No. I do not think so, but maybe I better improve my Ingleesh, you think? It is never wise to cross Antonio.'

No, she thought darkly, I'm sure. I'm sure he just loves it that way as well. He wasn't a man who struck her as being too forgiving.

They adjourned to the lounge for coffee, after an on-slaught of praise for Edna for the meal, which, as she cleared away the dishes, she took superbly in her stride, only stopping in her tracks to give Benjamin an I-told-you-so look, which he brushed aside with a wave of his hand.

She had not noticed him chatting much to Maria during the evening. Now, as they all moved off, Maria made a conscious effort to walk with him, holding his arm and talking and laughing a lot. Corinna thought that at least one of her deductions about the other woman had been spot-on. Maria came alive in the company of a man, any man. She spoke differently, held herself differently, laughed in a much louder voice.

Corinna was observing this when Antonio moved to stand next to her. They were the last to leave the dining-room, and when she would have made a hurried escape behind the general exodus, he held her back, his fingers piercing into her skin.

'I've been watching you,' he said tightly, 'and I don't like it.'

Corinna stared at him, bewildered. 'You don't like what?'

'I don't like the way you've been encouraging Roberto.'

She felt a sudden urge to level another of those angry kicks to his shin, and she only just managed to curb the desire.

'I wasn't encouraging Roberto,' she answered, her head suddenly as clear as a bell, but he carried on, as if she hadn't spoken.

'He's here to work, not to become involved with a pretty face who doesn't mind playing the field whenever it suits her.'

'What do you mean by that?'

'Work it out.' His face was derisive.

'I'd rather not.' She turned away, but he didn't release her.

'Well, shall I do it for you?' His eyes swept over her, and he said in a tight voice, 'You laugh with that smoky, come-hither look in your eyes, even though you've never seen Roberto in your life before this evening, you sit there while he drools all over you in that sexy little number, giving off all the right signals to a boy who has a girlfriend back in Italy...'

'You're exaggerating,' Corinna muttered uncomfortably, 'and I had no idea that he had a girlfriend. As far as I'm concerned, it was all a bit of harmless fun.'

'Harmless?' He shot her a disbelieving look. 'You? Harmless?'

She turned her head as though she'd been struck, and she heard him sigh, then his fingers touched her cheeks gently, making her stiffen.

'I...' he began stiffly, 'I shouldn't have said that— I—you bring out the worst in me, for reasons I can't comprehend.'

That was an apology, she thought in amazement, or as much of an apology as he was ever likely to utter, and she looked at him from under her lashes.

'I have feelings,' she said roughly.

'Yes,' he said, 'don't we all?' His hand dropped to his sides and he said shortly, 'But I need Roberto one hundred and ten per cent on his job when this subsidiary gets off the ground. I don't want his mind somewhere else.'

'Well, you can rest easy,' she replied wearily. 'I wasn't about to leap into bed with him.'

There was silence, and when she raised her eyes she saw that he was watching her broodingly, thinking things that she couldn't begin to guess.

'Have you ever leapt into bed with anybody?' he asked, his voice curious.

Her heart began to thud and she had a heavy, weak feeling in her knees.

'They're waiting for us through there,' she muttered, and he took not the slightest bit of notice of her attempt to change the subject.

'Roberto didn't really do anything for you, did he?' Antonio asked, and when she didn't reply, he continued in the same, speculative voice, 'You're the kind of girl who probably wouldn't gush all over a man she was seriously attracted to. Am I right?'

'Stop thinking that you can read me like a book!' she snapped, shying away from the thought that that was precisely what he was doing. She yanked her arm out of his fingers, to find that she was trembling. 'I think we'd better join the others, don't you? Before they send out a search party?'

'I think you're right,' he said in a strange voice. 'I think we had better join the others.' He turned abruptly on his heel and she found herself trailing into the room behind him, feeling shaken and a little disorientated.

The party now had that mellow atmosphere that all parties had when everyone was winding down, getting ready to leave, which they did after quite a bit of insistence on the part of Constance and her husband that dinner would be at their place next time.

Roberto, she noticed with some relief, abandoned his husky flirting. It was obvious that he was in awe of his boss, and as he said goodbye to her at the door, aware that Antonio was watching him, he gave a little rueful laugh and lightly told her to give him a call if she was ever in need of a friendly face.

Corinna smiled vaguely, knowing that that was hardly likely, and besides, what would his girlfriend think?

'Well,' Benjamin said as soon as the front door was shut behind the last guest, 'I'd forgotten what it was like socialising. Damned tiring for an old man like me.'

Corinna grinned, and Maria said ingratiatingly, 'You must have a good night's sleep.'

Benjamin didn't answer that. Corinna knew him well enough by now to see that he didn't like the other woman. He had been woodenly polite to her on the few occasions that he had addressed her, and Corinna could tell that given half a chance he would probably be on the phone arranging for her to stay somewhere else.

He ambled off to bed, insisting that Corinna not accompany him, and she was left there with Antonio and Maria, neither of whom she felt up to facing.

'I thought,' Maria said with a hard smile, 'that you and I might have a nightcap. We have not had much chance to chat, have we?' She turned to Antonio and tiptoed to kiss him on the mouth, a light fluttering kiss that, to Corinna's unskilled eyes, seemed to hold an invitation of more to come. 'Poor darling,' Maria said to Antonio with a pout, 'you look exhausted. You run up to bed and leave us to have a little girls' talk, no?'

'I have work to do,' he said by way of answering. He glanced at his watch. 'I'll be in the study.' He nodded curtly to Corinna and their eyes tangled, then she lowered hers nervously.

'Let us go to the lounge,' Maria said. She walked ahead with Antonio and Corinna was left bringing up the rear, feeling like a lamb going to the slaughter. She didn't want to have a girls' talk with Maria. She didn't want to have any kind of talk with her, for that matter, but she couldn't see how she could wriggle out of it without appearing churlish.

'So,' Maria said, as soon as they were in the lounge, 'you would like a liqueur.'

'No, thank you.'

'Oh yes, I forgot, you don't like it. Of course, now that we are alone, you can drop your little-girl act.'

'What did you want to talk to me about? I'm rather tired and I'd like to get to bed.'

Maria leisurely helped herself to a glass of scotch, moving to use the bar as though she had lived there all her life.

'Well, I will not keep you from your beauty sleep.' She sat on the sofa next to Corinna. Up close, Corinna could see that the other woman was older than she appeared from a distance and under forgiving lights. Probably in her early to mid-thirties. And despite the coyness whenever Antonio was around, there was a ruthless streak in her that was evident in the set of her mouth. Corinna thought that she probably did a damn good job running her parents' business. She and Antonio had a lot in common.

'It is about Antonio,' she said bluntly, and Corinna felt tell-tale colour creep into her cheeks. 'I have looked at you when he is around and you are infatuated with him. I know. A woman knows these things.'

'I am not!' Corinna protested loudly, 'and I can't believe you brought me in here to accuse me of something so stupid!' Her protestations sounded a little over-loud to her own ears, and she knew that she wasn't only denying the accusations to Maria, but also to that damned aggravating voice in her head.

'He has that effect,' Maria said with a cold smile. 'He is not an ordinary person. He stands out, no? But it will do you no good making eyes at him.'

Twice, Corinna thought, twice in one evening I've been accused of looking at someone. Whoever would have thought that I would have ever been seen as a *femme fatale*?

'You're quite wrong,' she denied heatedly. 'Not that it's any business of yours, anyway.'

'Oh, but it is my business!' The temperature in Maria's eyes, which had been frosty to start with, was dropping by the second. 'Maybe I should explain. He and I—how shall I put this? —have an understanding. We are not engaged, not in your formal English way, but we are destined for one another. You see, he heads one of the biggest pharmaceutical companies in Italy, much bigger than my parents', but a union of the two would make his position in the market unassailable. I am afraid that you are not in the right league to interest him.' She tried to turn the temperature up a bit so that the expression in her eyes now was one of semi-glacial sympathy. 'I am only telling you this, you understand, because I feel for you. After all, we are women together, all sisters under the skin.'

'Aren't we?' Corinna said through gritted teeth. If this was an example of sisterliness, then she was glad that she didn't have any siblings.

'Antonio,' Maria said, choosing her words carefully, 'thinks with his head and not with his heart.'

'You mean that he's not in love with you?'

Two bright spots of colour appeared on Maria's face. 'We have known each other for many years,' she said tightly. 'He is like a son to my parents.'

'Oh.' Corinna's voice implied that she was still waiting for an answer to her question.

'You are not his type,' Maria said bluntly. 'All that blonde English charm. It is not what he finds desirable. He likes his women hot-blooded. Hot-blooded and——' she paused on an indrawn breath '—intelligent.'

Corinna stood up, white-faced. 'I won't even ask what you're implying by that,' she said angrily.

'Oh, please,' Maria said, her eyes widening, 'I hope you are not offended. Perhaps I did not find the right word. My English, you know—there are gaps, sometimes I say the wrong thing in error...'

'If you'll excuse me, I really think I'll be getting off to bed now.'

'Of course. It is late. You must be tired.' Maria stood up, diminutive and deadly, and Corinna gave her a stony look. So it was war, was it? Over Antonio Silver! Ridiculous. She turned away and walked towards the door, not bothering with a backward glance.

Upstairs, in her bedroom, she sat down on the bed, and this time the reflection glimpsed in the mirror didn't throw back an image of a light-hearted, sexy woman. She looked spent and miserable, which was how she felt.

She didn't want to be attracted to Antonio but she had to face the fact that she was, and if Maria had spotted that after one day, then was he similarly aware of it? She listlessly washed her face, removed her fine garments, slipped into her nightgown, feeling like Cinderella after the carriage had once again become a pumpkin, then turned the light off, but she didn't go to sleep. She lay there, thinking, until she heard Maria's light footsteps, followed by Antonio's, and the low murmur of voices. She found her body tensing, and her thoughts went haywire, wondering what they were up to. Were they sleeping together? They might have a wonderful understanding, a business arrangement, he might be ruled by his head and not his heart, but he was a man, and a damned sexy one, and Maria Felucci was beautiful, brainy and, as she had made blatantly clear, available. The solution to that equation was transparently clear.

She dreaded waking up the following morning and having to deal with Antonio and Maria and her whole sorry plight, and she was surprised when Edna informed her, in the kitchen, that Maria had gone 'up town', which, translated, meant that she had gone to London where, Corinna thought, she was probably spending roughly the equivalent of her annual nursing income on a couple of outfits. And Benjamin, Edna continued, with some astonishment, was at the library, checking out computer manuals, whatever on earth for she, Edna, couldn't understand; after all, it was just like typing, wasn't it?

That, Corinna thought, only left Antonio, who was doubtless on his merry way to see how the office was coming along.

What was she going to do until Benjamin returned? A fleeting thought passed through her head: he doesn't really need me any more, and she felt, underneath the delight that she took in his growing independence, a certain degree of sadness.

The last person she felt equipped to facing pushed open the kitchen door just as she was finishing her coffee and said, 'You're here. Good. I want you to do some more work for me.'

She watched as he strolled across to the kitchen counter, poured himself a mug of coffee and proceeded to drink it, surveying her over the rim of the mug.

Her body was doing all the old familiar things, and her mind was going through the same tired routine of trying to stamp down her reaction to him. She gave him a cutting look.

'I take it that means that you can think of better things to do? Even though my father isn't around?'

'I *am* still employed by him, and we *are* still working on his historical piece of work.' Which, she thought, had rather taken a back seat ever since his son had shown up.

'Meet me in the study in five minutes,' he said, draining his mug, as if her protest had only confirmed that she had nothing better to do than his bidding.

She was tempted to leave him waiting in the study and to busy herself with something else in some other part of the house, but that, she knew, would have been waving a red rag to a bull, and she reluctantly finished her coffee and then walked towards the study, where he was sitting on the desk, waiting for her.

'What do you want me to do?' Corinna asked and, when he didn't answer, she looked up and reddened. His dark hair was combed away from his face, curling at the collar of his shirt, of which he had rolled the sleeves up to the elbows.

She couldn't sit down on the chair by the computer terminal because to do so would have brought her into direct contact with his thigh, so she remained where she was, hovering.

'Stop acting as though I'm disrupting your damned routine,' he said, surprising her by the vehemence in his voice, 'and close the door.' He lowered his eyes and began concentrating on the paperwork next to him, shuffling the documents restlessly through his fingers.

Corinna shut the door and returned to her hovering position.

'And stop hovering!' he commanded irritably.

'What do you want me to do?'

'Sit! Sit, dammit! Here!' He gestured to the chair which she had been studiously avoiding, and when he saw the expression on her face, he barked out, 'I won't bite! What's the matter?'

'Nothing.' She edged her way and perched nervously on the chair, wishing desperately that his leg weren't quite so close. Her eyes she kept glued to the computer screen.

'I didn't notice you skirting around Roberto last night,' he bit out. 'Oh, no, no modesty there.'

'He didn't spend the evening insulting me!' She stood up, and found that she was now really close to him, eye to eye, her skirt brushing against his trousers.

She was breathing heavily, her breasts rising and falling, her neat chignon more or less coming apart, which did nothing for her self-control.

'Well, no one's insulting you now.'

They stared at each other and she had a drowning sensation of being frozen in time, waiting for *something*. And as soon as it happened, she realised that that was just what she had been waiting for. Her mind must have stored up a hundred images of him, a thousand, and in some strange way it had put all those images together in such a way that she knew, as soon as his dark head bent towards hers, that her body had been longing desperately for his touch.

He put his hand behind her head and as his mouth moved over hers, hot and impatient, he unfastened her hair, groaning when it flowed loose over her shoulders.

Wherever common sense had migrated, she couldn't rescue it for the life of her. She felt swamped, utterly consumed by a craving to have him make love to her. She felt his tongue in her mouth and wound her arms around his head, caressing him, feeling his dark, springy hair between her fingers with intense pleasure.

When his hand found the small buttons of her blouse and began undoing them feverishly, she shuddered convulsively, offering her breasts to him, wanting him to find the taut nipples underneath her bra, which he did. He rubbed the peaks between his fingers and she moaned, arching back, her hands splayed on his arms. He was kissing her all over now, her face, her neck, moaning against her skin while his hands continued to caress her breasts, which seemed to have grown, spilling into his hands.

He parted her blouse and pushed up her bra then bent to take one nipple into his mouth.

She pressed his head against her, her breathing thick. Every pore in her body was reaching out to him and, as he hitched up her skirt, she raised her knee to the edge of the desk so that his fingers easily found the moistness between her parted thighs, exploring it until she felt as if she was going to explode.

It was only when he pulled back to look down at her that some of her carelessly discarded sanity began to return home. A wave of humiliation washed over her, but with his fingers still caressing the very depths of her, it receded for a while.

'I know Roberto did nothing for you,' he muttered. 'Your lips responded to him, but not your body.'

The hectic colour began to leave her face and she pulled back, aghast at herself. He didn't notice. Not to begin with. Not until she broke free and began getting her clothes back into order, aware that her fingers were making a damn bad job of it since they were shaking so much. Then he said huskily, 'No. Don't run away.'

'I can't do any work for you,' she muttered.

'Dammit, Corinna, I know what's behind that sober look you try so hard to cultivate. I know I turn you on. I want to make love to you. Right here and right now.'

Already she was backing away, busily rebuttoning her blouse, eyeing him as if he were some dangerous jungle animal that might strike again at any moment.

She hated herself. He knew that he turned her on. Well, she thought hysterically, how could he fail to? His girlfriend, lover, whatever, had spotted it at a glance, hadn't she?

'This was a mistake.' The words tumbled out of her mouth. 'Leave me alone! I don't want you or any other man!'

He advanced on her and gripped her shoulders. 'Why are you so afraid?'

'Leave me alone!' Her voice had at least returned to something resembling normality, now that she was no longer in a state of semi-undress.

'No!'

She wriggled free and fled to the door, opening it and then speaking over her shoulder.

'And I don't want you ever to touch me again!' Then, before he could speak, she slammed the door behind her and rushed up to her bedroom, taking the stairs two at a time, thanking God that Benjamin wasn't around to hear the desperate pounding of her steps.

# CHAPTER SEVEN

THE blood was pounding in her head, drowning out the sounds of anything else. If she had encountered anyone on the landing, she would probably have flown past them without seeing them.

Her mind was consumed with pictures of Antonio. She hadn't realised how much her brain had stored up, how many images there were waiting to accost her the minute she gave them the chance.

Deanbridge House, which for so long had been her haven, a little oasis of peace in a troubled world, now assumed the dimensions of a nightmare. She couldn't move, she couldn't breathe, without being aware of the fact that she might bump into Antonio, that he might be anywhere, dark, good-looking, unhinging her every time she laid eyes on him.

Maria's presence was an additional complication. Corinna wasn't intimidated by her, but, she thought now, out of breath when she finally reached her bedroom door, it was just something else, wasn't it?

She shut the bedroom door and walked towards the bed. Her body felt limp and despairing. She closed her eyes and placed her linked fingers over them, and still the thoughts assaulted her from all angles. The stupidity of her emotions, the sheer folly of being attracted to a man like Antonio Silver. It was as if, mentally exhausted from having lived cautiously, from never having taken risks, her mind had finally rebelled and left her defenceless against someone like him.

Of all the men in the world, she groaned inwardly, why him? Why did her body have to choose him as the recipient of her twenty-three years of untested sexuality? He was one of life's users when it came to women. He flicked a finger and they fell at his feet. She wanted stability out of a relationship, security, for heaven's sake! She couldn't have done worse if she had strolled down to the local prison and selected one of its inmates.

From as far back as she could remember, she had cautioned herself that life was not about thunderbolts and lightning. It was about peace and contentment and not having to live constantly hanging on to the edge of your seat. So where had all the good caution gone when she needed it? Through the window, she thought bitterly. Good sense had reared up like a wayward horse, breaking free of its reins and hurtling through the barn door, and she had a dismal feeling that that barn door was never going to be repaired.

Ever since he had walked through the front door, she had been at war with herself. Every confrontation with him had been an internal battle, with her head telling her one thing, and her emotions telling her something quite different, and she felt totally spent.

Perhaps, she thought, she should just leave, hand in her resignation, then she thought of Benjamin, of his possible disappointment, and she felt like a trapped animal with nowhere much to run.

Most girls, she realised, could count on their mothers for sympathy, but this was a solution to which she had no recourse. Divorce had embittered her mother against men. She had approved of Michael because he was bland and controllable, but she would hate Antonio and she would have no sympathy for her daughter.

Corinna wasn't even aware of another presence in the bedroom until Antonio spoke, then she sat up, horrified, staring at him with huge eyes as if an alien had suddenly beamed itself into the room.

'What are you doing here?' she asked, while her thoughts whirled back into their various cubbyholes. 'You can't just breeze into my bedroom as if you had some kind of right!' She was propping herself up on her hands, which felt as though they were going to buckle under at any moment.

Antonio walked into the room slowly, his eyes on her face, but he didn't come near her. He strolled across to the window to stare out, his hands in his pockets, and she watched him with a dreadful, urgent compulsion.

'Get out!' she said, finding her voice.

He turned to face her, perching on the edge of the window ledge. 'No. Not until you've told me what the hell all that was about.'

'I don't want to talk about it.'

'Well, I do!'

'Fine, then talk about it to yourself.'

That was the wrong response. He moved towards her and sat on the bed. His face was savage, his eyes narrowed to silver slits.

'I realise that——' he raked his fingers through his hair and shook his head impatiently '—that you've had a broken love-affair, but you act as though you're frightened of life.'

'I just don't want involvement with anyone.'

'Why not? Did he mean that much to you?'

She raised her eyes to his and made an effort to appear controlled. 'It's none of your business,' she said stubbornly.

'It damn well is when you throw a bucket of cold water over me every time you feel yourself getting aroused!'

'Oh, well, I'm so sorry I can't fall in with your ex- pectations for every woman to be eternally obliging with you. And have you forgotten that you already have a girlfriend?'

'Maria isn't my girlfriend,' he said bluntly.

'Well, you've obviously kept that information to yourself, because she happens to think that that's precisely what she is.'

'And does that make you jealous?' His voice was husky and she thought, Oh, that would really appeal to you, wouldn't it? Two women clamouring for your scraps of attention?

'She's welcome to you.'

His mouth hardened. 'That's not what your body says whenever I touch it.'

The fact that she couldn't reasonably deny that only made her angrier.

'I am not interested in sex!' she said heatedly, and then flushed in confusion as his eyes scoured her.

'You damn well are! You might not have been with that ex-boyfriend of yours, but maybe that's why you decided to walk out on the relationship. Am I right?'

'Stop putting words into my mouth!'

'Then start answering me when I talk to you!' His eyes raked over her with savage intensity.

He wasn't going to go, she thought wearily. Going wasn't his style, was it, not when it didn't suit him? He had wanted her and she had frozen him out and now he wanted to know why. He would sit there, she knew, hammering away at her until he got what he wanted. She sighed tiredly, and said, 'All right. You want answers; here are some answers. I can't and won't make love to you because what you have to offer isn't enough.'

His eyes became icy. 'What I have to offer?'

'I have no desire to become a number! I've never been that sort of girl, out for a good time, never mind the consequences. If you must know, my parents had a very protracted, bitter divorce and I don't see the point in any relationship with a man unless...'

There was dawning comprehension in his eyes. 'You want commitment, is that it?' he asked harshly, and she didn't say anything.

It sounded Victorian, but that didn't change the fact that that was the way she felt. She could never make love with someone on a passing whim. Many of her friends did. They slept with their boyfriends, broke off with them, replaced them with new boyfriends, in a seemingly never-ending circle, and Corinna had listened to their tales of woe with a mixture of sympathy and incomprehension. I have Michael she had always thought, not bothering to ask herself why she had never made love to him even though the commitment was there.

Now she knew why. She had never been in love with him. But she was in love with Antonio Silver, desperately, hopelessly, pointlessly in love with him and that was the real reason why, however much her body clamoured for fulfilment, her heart told her that she would be a fool to accept anything less than marriage.

She lowered her eyes, suddenly feeling slightly ill. Not just physical attraction, she thought with a drowning sense of panic, but love, the whole works, the hook, the line and the sinker. I've swallowed the lot.

Her body went hot, then cold. She felt faint.

'Commitment is no guarantee of a lasting marriage,' Antonio said harshly. 'Wake up. Life is all about chances, gambles. So you had problems with your parents. I sympathise. You might care to remember that my life hasn't exactly been one sweet-smelling bed of roses as far as my parents were concerned.' She wasn't looking at him, preferring to concentrate her attention on her hands rather than face the brilliant glitter of his eyes. He coiled his long fingers into her hair and forced her head up.

'I know that,' she mumbled.

'In this day and age, divorce is a fact of life. You're telling me that you're allowing it to continue sinking its teeth into everything you do and think.'

'That's not what I'm saying, and kindly remove your hands from my hair; you're hurting me.'

'Tough,' Antonio said grimly.

Corinna was finding it difficult to breathe. His face was only inches away from her own. If she reached out, she would be able to trace the sensuous curve of his mouth, the powerful line of his jaw.

'Sex doesn't entail security and everlasting happiness,' he rasped. 'Don't tell me that you're so naïve that you don't understand that.'

Her eyes flashed coldly. 'I prefer to be naïve than to be like you, cynical.'

He flushed darkly at that. 'I'm a realist. I enjoy women but commitment is a complication. I'm afraid, my sweet, that however sexy I find you and however much I'm attracted to you, it's not an option I can offer.' He released her but she remained staring at him, straining forward, her eyes intent.

'I never asked you to,' she said finally.

He gave her a crooked smile. 'No, you didn't, did you?'

He wasn't touching her, but she felt as though he were, as though his fingers were caressing her face, her lips, her body.

'Wouldn't that boyfriend of yours give you the security you needed? Was that why you broke off with him?'

'Does it matter?' Corinna asked in a low voice. He waited, silently, and eventually she said, 'He did offer me security, as a matter of fact. He wanted marriage, kids, everything, but...'

'But it was unexciting?'

She shrugged, and his eyes darkened fractionally.

'What do you think I'm trying to tell you?' he asked, and the deep warmth in his voice alarmed her. 'You can't plot the course of your life; you can't reach out and pick security from a tree like an apple.' He touched her face and she stared at him with panic. 'You want security, you want commitment, yet when it's offered you turn it down. I really don't think you have a clue as to what you want. But if it's excitement——' he gave a low laugh '—I can give you that. Believe me, I can make you feel things that you never knew existed.' He was making love to her with his eyes, with the husky murmur of his voice.

His hand moved along her collarbone, then over one aching breast, and she gasped.

'I don't want excitement,' she said weakly, 'I want...' But she couldn't think clearly. What did she want? He had been right when he said that the security which she had craved, once offered, had been unappealing, but he had missed the most important point. It had been unappealing because there had been no love there. His parents' divorce had jaded him, had jaundiced his views of marriage, while her own parents' divorce had had just the opposite effect. It had made her yearn for an impossible plateau of contentment, where bitterness and remorse couldn't exist.

There was, she realised, no such place, but contentment was a second-best emotion anyway, she thought, compared to the exquisite agony of love.

Now he was telling her that sex was what he could give her, and she drew back from him, frozen.

'This isn't getting either of us anywhere,' she muttered, and with an oath he stood up and began moving restlessly around the room, before standing in front of her.

'I'm not about to offer you marriage,' he said tersely.
'I see no need for the pair of slippers in front of the fire,
while the little lady cooks up something tasty in the
kitchen.'

'This is the twentieth century! I don't think that
slippers in front of a fire and the little lady scurrying
around in the kitchen is exactly an accurate picture of
your average household!'

'Well, whatever the picture is, I'm having none of it.'
He smiled, a cool, mocking smile. 'But my offer still
stands.'

'Offer? What offer?'

'Excitement, my dear Corinna.' He leaned over,
placing his hands on either side of her. Without warning,
his hand slid to cup her breast and she felt it harden
against his palm. 'I want you and you want me, and
sooner or later you'll succumb.'

'Why?' she asked, breathing quickly. She made an attempt to push his hand away and he reached out quickly
to propel her flat on the bed, pinning her hands above
her head with his free arm. He was almost on top of
her. She could feel the weight of his body, the hardness
of his thighs against hers, and most of all the steady
caress of her breast, which ached with pleasure.

His voice was calm enough, but his eyes were hot and
feverish. His hand moved to her flat stomach and he
stroked her bare skin underneath the shirt.

'I'm not one of your women,' she said, thinking that
that was a joke. She wanted him, she loved him; what
else was she, for heaven's sake?

'Think it over.' He stood up and she jerked back on
the bed.

'I can give you my answer right now!'

He smiled, but there was no real amusement there.
She watched in silence as he walked towards the door,

opened it, and then let himself out. Then she fell back on the bed, trembling.

She should never have let him see that she was atracted to him. That had been her first great mistake. He was a man who moved with confidence, spoke with confidence. His power, his looks, his considerable charm had not inured him to the possibility of a woman to whom he was attracted not responding. If she had made it clear from the start that she wasn't interested, then he would have given up the pursuit. He would have simply shrugged his shoulders in that way of his and walked away. He didn't strike her as a man who kept running when the signals weren't bright green.

But she had responded to him. She had let him see that chink in her, a chink which she hadn't even known existed because it was the one aspect in her life for which she had not bargained, and of course, he had smiled and assumed the inevitable.

She should, she knew now, have steeled herself against that powerful armoury of sexual weapons which were at his disposal, and consoled herself with the thought that if she had been stupid enough to be attracted to him, to fall in love with him no less, then time would take care of that. Time took care of everything. She had met and nursed people who had lain in their hospital beds, aware that they were dying, and slowly, over time, coming to terms with it until it became a more or less accepted fact. Once they had accepted it, they began to cope.

Time would have healed her stupid heart, and how much easier it would have been if she had turned her back on him and not let him see the glimmer of sexual arousal on her face.

Perhaps, she reasoned brightly, he wouldn't be around for much longer. Certainly he had made an awful lot of progress since he had first arrived. The office space had been sorted out, skeleton staff had been employed, and of course, more important than any of that, the rift between himself and his father, slow to heal, was gradually repairing itself.

Then there was the question of Maria. Sooner or later, she would have to return to Italy. She might be crazy about Antonio, crazy enough to have followed him across to England even when she must have known, deep down, that she was not his fiancée, despite what she had said to the contrary, but she would shortly have to return to this all-important job which she was so fond of talking about. She telephoned her office daily, assuring Benjamin that she would of course settle the phone bill before she left, and she always made sure that everyone knew just how much her presence was missed in her company. That being the case, she was hardly going to extend her stay much longer. And if she left, she would only very reluctantly leave Antonio behind. When it came to men, Maria was a fighter.

He wasn't someone who could be told or even persuaded to do anything he didn't want to, and if he was not a man who wanted love and romance, then perhaps Maria had been close to truth when she said that she and Antonio had a business arrangement, an understanding, that stretched beyond flowers and sweet nothings. Maybe now he would decide that a marriage of convenience was really a highly intelligent move.

Maybe, she thought, she should seriously consider taking some time off. Not resigning, but a few weeks, enough time to escape the nerve-racking presence of Antonio.

In truth, she had had an awful lot of free time on her hands recently, with Benjamin's sudden burst of independence. She had written a lot of letters, some of which were still waiting on the hallway table to be posted, still did her daily chores with Benjamin, but did he really need her the way that he had when she had first arrived?

The questions were running round and round in her head, looking for answers, when there was a knock on the door and she stiffened. If it was Antonio, she had nothing further to say to him, but the chances were it was Benjamin, returned from his merry exploits in the newly discovered Outside World.

She called 'Come in!' without actually moving from the bed, and Maria walked in, looking like a million dollars in a pair of silk culottes and a matching silk camisole, both ivory-coloured, which made her dark looks even more striking.

Corinna sat up abruptly and slipped her legs off the edge of the bed. As usual when she was with Maria, she felt as though she should be prepared to go to war.

Maria looked at her coldly and said, 'There's no need to get up. I won't be long. I have only come to say one thing to you: keep away from Antonio.'

'We've already been over this old ground,' Corinna returned coldly. 'It's beginning to get boring.'

Maria's scarlet lips tightened. 'How would you know what is boring and what is not?' she said, and her lips were pulled back in a snarl, 'you who sit here tending an old man, no life outside this mausoleum of a house.'

'I know enough about it to tell you that constantly trying to drum it into my head that Antonio is your personal property isn't exciting conversation.'

This was ludicrous. She felt exhausted after Antonio and in no mood to humour Maria by biting her lips in order to avoid a fight. Right now, Corinna thought, I'm in the right frame of mind for all-out war.

'Can you not find a man? Someone more like you? Antonio is not like you; he is in a different league.'

'So you've already told me,' Corinna said coldly. 'Your league, I assume?'

'That is correct.' The claws were definitely out now. Maria's face was white like marble and her black eyes were like stones.

'In that case, you have nothing to fear from me, have you?'

There was nonplussed silence.

'Leave him alone,' Maria spat out eventually. 'Leave him alone or you will be sorry.'

'Is that a threat?'

'It is whatever you want to make of it.' She turned on her heel and left the bedroom, her back stiff.

# CHAPTER EIGHT

CORINNA saw nothing at all of either Antonio or Maria on the Saturday evening, and on the Sunday she made sure that she kept as far away from them both as she possibly could. Over lunch, when she couldn't achieve that, she maintained a polite front, smiling when she had to, but mostly making sure that she appeared normal.

Normal, though, was something that she didn't feel she was ever going to be again. Normal had been that distant time before Antonio had walked into her life and thrown it upside down. Even the despondency she had felt at the end of her active nursing career in hospital, and when she had ended her relationship with Michael, paled in comparison with what she was going through now.

Nobody had ever warned her that love hurt, really hurt. It hurt just watching Antonio, greedily and surreptitiously looking at the way he moved, the things he did, hearing his deep, controlled, ironic voice with a shiver of awareness that no amount of stern reasoning to herself could dispel.

Maria she tried to ignore completely. Despite the other woman's threats, there was, Corinna suspected, precious little she could actually do to her. A duel at dawn? A fist fight? It was ludicrous, but she still didn't care for the cold, hard gleam of those eyes, or the cruelty of that mouth.

She was entering the lounge, clutching her book in front of her so that if Antonio did happen to be in there she could subside into some faraway sofa, whip it out and hide behind it, when Benjamin beckoned her across with a conspiratorial wave of the hand and told her to sit down.

'Guess what,' he said brightly, 'the dragon is about to leave.'

'The dragon?'

'Maria.'

'Is she?' This was news to Corinna. Nothing had been said over lunch, but probably neither Maria nor Antonio considered that piece of information to be relevant to her.

'In two days' time. Says the company can't do without her any longer, but I think there's another reason.'

'I'm sure,' Corinna said wryly. 'You have the knack of seeing ulterior motives behind the most innocent actions.'

'I could be offended at that, young lady,' Benjamin said, sniffing, and she laughed with genuine amusement at his expression. 'I think,' he whispered, so that she was tempted to remind him that he was in his own house, and not obliged to keep his voice low if he didn't want to, '*I* think that she's being seen off the premises by my son.'

Corinna lowered her eyes. 'I'm sure you're wrong,' she said calmly.

'Well, when they told me that a short while ago, he didn't seem too grieved over her imminent departure.'

Corinna stood up and began straightening up the lounge. Activity was the only thing she could think of to hide her feelings at this bit of news. If Maria was leaving, she thought, then Antonio would be as well. If not immediately, then quite soon, and the prospect of that, which she knew should fill her with joy, was similar to seeing a large, black, never-ending hole gaping in front of her.

No more Antonio. It was stupid not to be happy at that. It was also immensely stupid to acknowledge that the highs and lows which she associated with him, that keen alertness which she felt whenever he was around, might be painful, but were infinitely better than the void which she now foresaw for herself.

'Benjamin,' she said slowly, 'I don't mean to change the subject, but I've been thinking that perhaps I could have some time off work.' She heard a slight noise from the door, and looked around to see Maria standing there. She ignored her. 'A short holiday, perhaps somewhere hot.'

'Why?' Benjamin demanded, squinting at her and looking at her as if she had just announced a desire to fly to the moon. 'Heat doesn't agree with you. Besides, it's been quite warm over here this summer.'

'Well, then, perhaps somewhere cold.'

'Where?'

Anywhere, she felt like confessing. Siberia, Outer Mongolia, Timbuctoo, anywhere. But Maria had now entered the lounge and had sat down on one of the sofas, flicking through a magazine.

'Wherever.'

'Hm.' He gave that some thought, then said grudgingly, 'It's been a while since you had a break. Who knows? Might perk you up. You've been looking down in the dumps lately. Don't know why, do you?'

That was a line Corinna definitely didn't wish to pursue, especially not with Maria within earshot, supposedly wrapped up in the magazine but probably all ears. She muttered something about him giving it some thought as to when it would be convenient for her to take a couple of weeks off, and then she changed the subject altogether.

She walked across to sit down, leaving Benjamin to continue devouring the Sunday newspapers in peace, and she realised with some shock that Maria was smiling at her. Actually smiling. Not one of those ghastly, reptilian efforts that had made her so wary in the past, but a genuine smile.

'Come and sit by me,' she said, gesturing to the space next to her on the sofa, and Corinna hesitatingly obliged.

Her instincts told her not to throw caution completely to the four winds, but her nature was such that she found it difficult to maintain any sort of hostility in the face of overt friendliness.

'I just want to say,' Maria murmured, 'how silly I've been ever since I arrived here at Deanbridge House.'

Corinna's eyes opened wide. 'You do?' This was as unbelievable as if Maria had announced that she was shedding her power suits and going to live in a commune.

'Yes,' she said, still smiling, although there was something a little rueful about the smile now. 'The fact is that I came over here on a wild-goose chase.' She sighed deeply. 'Let me explain.' She paused, trying to find the right words to express herself. With an unconscious gesture, she brushed some of her neatly tailored hair behind one ear. 'Antonio and I—well, I always thought that we would be married. Not just because it would have brought our two companies together, or even because my parents seemed to expect it, but because I felt that there was something else there. Some attraction between us. I was wrong. I've only really had to recognise that since coming over here, although maybe I had known it already, deep down, the way a woman knows.' She stopped, looking to Corinna to share that feeling, and Corinna nodded. 'Antonio isn't made for love,'

Maria said sadly. 'He likes his independence, his power, his freedom, too much to give any of it away by falling in love. And me, well, let us just say, between women, that love is an important aspect of marriage, is it not?'

'Oh, yes,' Corinna said with some feeling.

'Yes. So I have decided to go away. I do not know if you have been told, but I am leaving tomorrow, early evening I believe.'

Corinna nodded. 'Benjamin told me, yes.'

Maria looked across the room to where he was sitting behind a newspaper, the business section of the *Sunday Times*, and she said a little anxiously, 'He cannot hear us, can he?'

Corinna shook her head. 'No. It would take a full-scale war in this lounge to tear his attention away from the Sunday papers.'

'Because this is—how do you English call it? Girls' talk.' Maria looked relieved.

'Well, I'm sorry that things didn't work out for you,' Corinna said awkwardly. 'I'm sure you'll meet someone in Italy.'

'Doubtless.' Maria gazed down at the slender, brown fingers, which were splayed out on her lap. 'But it leaves the field open for you, no?'

Corinna went red and didn't say anything. It was odd having this conversation with the other woman. Unbelievable, dreamlike. She wouldn't have thought that Maria would have been anything other than hostile towards her, but yet here she was, pouring her heart out, reaching for sympathy.

'Well,' Maria continued, a little more briskly, though there was a shimmer of tears in her eyes, 'that is all I wanted to say, and I am so sorry I did not say it sooner. I feel we could have been friends. Women should be friends to each other, I feel. We are all sisters under the skin, are we not?'

Corinna nodded. She was sure that she had heard that phrase used before.

'Now, I go to pack. Thank you for listening to me.' The sad smile was back on Maria's lovely face as she stood up, straightening her skirt, smoothing it down over her slim hips and flat stomach.

She left the room and Benjamin didn't even look up. He was still absorbed behind the newspaper. In a minute, he would probably make some cryptic remark about something he'd read, knowing that Corinna was still in the room, but he wouldn't expect a response. He would immediately carry on reading. She decided to go upstairs, have a bath, think about what Maria had told her.

Perhaps, she thought, walking into the hallway, perhaps she had misjudged the other woman. It was easy to get trapped behind a wall of silly muddles and complications. Maybe if she'd not been quite so defensive to start with, they might have been on more friendly terms from the start. She uneasily remembered those jet-black, stone-hard eyes. Perhaps not.

She was lost in her thoughts. The last person she expected to see was Antonio, and in fact she didn't. It was only when she felt the pressure of his fingers on her arm that she became aware of his presence alongside her.

'I want to talk to you,' he said, turning her to face him. It was obvious that he had just had a shower. His hair was still damp and combed back so that every line of that harsh, powerful face was thrown into striking focus. She could smell that clean, male smell and it filled her nostrils, making her a little giddy.

'What about?' she asked, stepping back a little as he released her.

'I don't want to talk here,' he said tersely, ignoring her question. 'Let's go into the study.'

'I'd rather not,' Corinna replied, thinking that confinement with Antonio Silver was the one thing she didn't want. In fact, the one thing she had been avoiding all weekend.

'Why?' he jeered softly. 'Do you think I might attack you? I'll keep my hands to myself, you needn't worry.'

'I wasn't worried about that,' she answered, feeling more nervous by the minute. 'I just don't know what we could possibly have to talk about.'

He didn't answer. He walked off in the direction of the study and, with a sigh of intense frustration, she found herself following him. Sometimes, when she had thought about that arrogant confidence of his, she had found it amusing. Right now, she found it alarming. What was it about this man that could draw people like a magnet?

As soon as they were inside the study, he shut the door behind her and leaned against it, looking at her, his arms folded.

'I've been thinking about what we discussed.' His lips twisted and he looked down in apparent fascination at the tip of his shoe.

'What we discussed?'

'You know what I'm talking about!'

'If I did, I wouldn't ask. Apart from anything else, I didn't think that we ever discussed things. I thought we argued.'

'You're being pedantic.' He unfolded his arms to rake his long fingers through his hair. There was something restless about his movements. She felt that rather than heard it in his voice.

'I went away and thought about what you said about commitment.'

'Oh.' Her heart skipped a beat and a little seed of hope took root and began to grow. Small but insistent. She tried to still it, but it ticked away inside her, until her legs felt so weak that she thought she would fall if she didn't sit down. She took a few steps towards the desk and perched on the edge of it.

'I've told Maria that she had to leave,' Antonio said heavily, staring at her from under thick fringed lashes. 'I should have told her so from the start, from the moment she set foot through that front door, but it didn't seem necessary. I really thought that if I told her I just wasn't interested, she would get the message and leave, but she didn't. Told me she was important to me, which, of course——' his voice was derisory now, '—she isn't, company or no company.'

Corinna frowned. This was a slightly different version about Maria's imminent departure, wasn't it? Perhaps Maria had fabricated hers to salvage some of her pride. That would be understandable. She found that she desperately wanted to believe Antonio, desperately wanted him to say those few words that would have her rushing into his arms. Whoever said that some fairy-tales couldn't come true?

He walked towards her and placed his hands on the desk on either side of her, imprisoning her, and her heart skipped another hopeful beat.

He hadn't been looking at her directly before, but he was now. Straight into her eyes. Hypnotic, she thought. Those steel-grey eyes were the eyes of a hypnotist.

'I won't be over here for much longer,' he said. 'If everything goes according to plan, and there's no reason why it shouldn't, then I'll be here another week. Maybe less. Roberto will take over from me, and my father of course.'

'He'll miss you.'

Antonio nodded, but she could see that his thoughts weren't on that at all.

'Would you?' he asked in a voice that was so low that she had to strain to decipher the words.

'We all will,' she replied, looking down. She could feel a faint film of perspiration covering her body.

'I didn't ask that. I asked if *you* would. Answer me. Would *you* miss me if I left?'

'I have no idea,' she heard herself mumble.

'Good,' he said, as though his question had been met with a vigorous nod of the head and shouts of Yes, yes, yes! His hand reached up to stroke her cheek and she held her breath in nervous expectation. 'Because I would miss you. I've never had to say that to a woman before, any woman. Never. So I'm asking you to come back with me to Italy. I know it would mean leaving your family behind, but we would come back to England regularly. Several times in a year.'

'Are you asking me . . . ?'

'To be my mistress.'

It took a few seconds for his words to sink in, then it was as though she had been flying one minute, high above the clouds on silver wings, only to find herself plummeting down back to earth.

He wanted her and he was prepared to live with her, but not to marry her, and she had a wild, raging impulse to hit him, but she controlled herself and forced her lips into a wooden smile.

'Thank you so much for your kind offer,' she said politely, 'but I'm afraid not.'

She levered herself off the desk and tried to push past him, but he forced her back.

'Why not?' he demanded. 'You spent long enough talking about commitment. Well, I'm prepared to live with you, isn't that commitment enough?'

'Not for me,' she said quietly.

'It's more than I've ever offered anyone.' He gave her a look of baffled anger.

'In that case, I'm sure you won't have any trouble finding someone else to take you up on your offer. Now please could you let me go?'

'No!' he roared, as his anger erupted into volcanic, uncomprehending fury, 'I damn well could not! What the hell's the matter with you? Marriage isn't for me, so I offer you the next best thing. In fact, a lot of people would say that cohabitation is better than marriage!'

'Would they? Well, a lot of people are entitled to their opinion.' That remark seemed to infuriate him further.

'But you're different,' he said harshly, 'is that it?'

'Different enough to know what I don't want, and top of that list is moving into some apartment with you as your kept woman.'

'Don't you adopt that tone of voice with me! You act as though I've insulted you.'

'You have!'

'Don't be ridiculous.' He lowered his eyes, then smiled at her, a smile full of potent, lethal charm. 'It makes sense. You can't deny we're attracted to each other. You've made it clear that you don't want a one-month fling; well, then, move in with me. It's as permanent as I'll ever get.'

She wished that she could be as casual as he was. Move in. Make love. When that's over and done with, no problem, you just move out. No ties, no strings, no real attachment.

She didn't doubt that for him it was a wildly generous offer. She didn't doubt that it was an offer he had never made to any woman before. He had probably never had to, because no one had ever refused him. She had, though, and perhaps that had fuelled his own attraction to her. But attraction or not, he wasn't stupid, and he wasn't about to get in over his head with a woman just because he fancied her.

'Can I go now?' she asked in that same flat, expressionless voice which she couldn't help, but which was like waving a red rag to a bull.

His hand flicked out and he cupped her face, tilting it up to his.

'You're so steeped in your damn meaningless priorities—well, deny this.' His head swooped down and his lips hit hers with angry force. She wriggled against him but she couldn't do a thing to escape, and for a while she did her best not to respond to him. She remained quite still, giving no sign of returning his kiss, and if he had continued trying to force her to co-operate, she almost certainly would have won the battle she was fighting with herself, but he was an expert. His hand found her spine and traced a line along it, sending a little shudder running through her, and his lips abandoned their hungry demand.

Instead, he kissed her gently, coaxingly, teasing her lips with his tongue.

'This isn't fair,' she muttered, parting her lips, and he laughed against her mouth.

'What in life ever is?'

'You're not going to get me to Italy by doing this, by trying to seduce me,' she said on a shaky breath, and both his arms reached behind her, drawing her close to him, so close that she could feel him hard and aroused against her.

'No,' he agreed.

'You won't prove anything except that you're stronger than I am.'

She desperately would have liked to sound indignant, and she heard the excitement in her voice with panic.

'I'm not out to prove a thing,' he said silkily. She was wearing a loose dress, which he unzipped at the back, then he unhooked her bra and, freed of their restraint, her breasts hung heavy and aching.

This, she realised, was the third time that he had touched her, beckoned her, and for the third time she had obeyed, even though she had spent hours, days, rallying her forces to defend her from this very onslaught. There seemed little point in telling herself that she was behaving with a dangerous lack of foresight. Danger, when he was touching her like this, became an irresistible temptation.

He shrugged off his shirt, without seeming to release her at all, then he walked across to the study door and locked it.

She watched him avidly, taking in the long lines of his back, the broad shoulders, the slim hips and shivered compulsively.

He smiled as he walked back to her and there was an ironic awareness in his smile. She was fascinated by him, by the sheer magnificence of his body, and he saw that and was amused by it.

He placed his hands on her shoulders and sprinkled her face with delicate little kisses that made her close her eyes and smile. Then he eased her dress along her shoulders, very slowly, taking his time, until it fell in a pool around her feet. This was followed by the remainder of her underclothes, and she stepped out of her shoes. Now she was completely naked and, mysteriously, she didn't feel at all exposed or uncomfortable.

There was pleasure in his eyes when they met hers.

'You're beautiful,' he murmured, trailing his finger between her breasts and down to her navel, where it circled tantalisingly for a few seconds.

He undressed completely and then said with a wry grimace, 'Not the ideal place for making love.' His eyes flicked towards her and she could read uncertainty there. Was she going to back out like the last time?

She knew that she wasn't. She wanted him and it felt right, absolutely right, to be surrendering herself for the first time to the man she was madly in love with. She wasn't about to embark on an affair with him, she wasn't going to hop on a plane and jet off to a rented apartment where she would stay until he grew bored with her. But why shouldn't she, she thought a little wildly, give in to this overwhelming need in her just this once? Why shouldn't she allow herself this memory to keep her warm at night in the years to come? If she never made love to him, then wouldn't she forever wonder what it would have been like?

She was tired of thinking of consequences.

He read the expression of willing compliance on her face and moaned huskily, then he kissed her, and this time it was with a possessive, feverish hunger that echoed her own. He reached down to hold her buttocks in his hands, pressing her against him.

When his kisses moved to her neck, she arched back, inviting him to explore her further.

Somewhere, deep inside her, an explosion was waiting to happen.

He lowered himself gradually along her, sucking her nipples, licking the ripe fullness of her breasts, massaging them with his hands so that they were like fruit ready to be tasted.

And he lingered on them, caressing them with easy, expert touches, arousing her to that explosion inside.

She moaned and then gasped as his mouth found other sensitive areas.

When he finally straightened up, it was to pull her legs around his waist, then he gently eased himself in, letting her dictate the pace and only thrusting harder when she was ready.

Corinna had never really thought about sex. It was a light-hearted subject bandied about amid much laughter by her girl friends. It had occurred to her that it might not be a marvellous experience the first time, and the fact that she had never really been attracted to Michael, however fond she had been of him, subconsciously fuelled that unspoken assumption. It had never crossed her mind that she would find herself swept off to dizzy, unexplored heights that would make her eager for more.

She touched him now, tentatively at first, then with growing confidence as she felt his body respond to her and heard his deep moans of growing pleasure.

'There are better places than this...' he muttered into her ear and she laughed.

'Are there? This seems fine to me.'

'You're a wanton woman.'

'Aren't I?' Corinna murmured, half shocked at her behaviour. She kissed him on the mouth, thrusting her tongue to explore, and he pulled her against him, his hands gripping the small of her back.

They slid to the ground, on to her crumpled bundle of clothes, and this time she pushed him back, kissing his neck, running her hands along the lean, powerful lines of his body.

She could feel every muscle under his skin. She caressed his shoulders, then stroked the hard, flat planes of his stomach with the flat of her hand. As she touched his manhood, she felt an intense wave of desire wash over her, and he covered her hand with his own, guiding her until she fell into an easy rhythm.

'You witch,' he said, breathing heavily, and she smiled, not stopping her action, wanting to explore every intimate part of his body.

She covered his body with her own, and he cupped her breasts with his hands, arching up to lick the sensitive peaks, which were hard and tingling.

Her eyes were closed, her head thrown back, with her long, fair hair spilling over her back and forming a gold curtain which hung to one side.

The sound of them making love filled the study and she gave a small sigh of utter bliss.

She moved quickly against him and he fell back with a groan as they spiralled together towards climax.

Afterwards, she lay alongside him, with their legs entwined. His eyes were half closed, and she looked at him, at his graceful, powerful body, the harsh lines of his face, that expressive mouth that could be forbidding or erotically sensual. She would have liked to tell him how much she loved him, but she realised immediately that she couldn't. There were some things that were far better left unsaid, and she knew that declarations of love fell into this category.

For the moment it was enough that he wanted her.

He looked at her and she hurriedly looked down, only raising her eyes to meet his when she was sure that they would not betray her.

'So,' he said lazily, running his finger along her spine. It was like a series of tiny, electrical shocks. 'Where do we go from here?'

'To our respective bedrooms,' she said, lying flat on her back and flinging one arm above her head. 'We can't spend the night here, after all. Edna would go berserk if she discovered us asleep. She'd have a heart attack on the spot.' She knew that that was not his question, but she wanted to have some time to think, to put her life into some kind of perspective, now that its course had been altered so dramatically and irrevocably.

How could things ever be the same again? How could she ever wake up in the morning and feel the same pleasant anticipation of a life that held no surprises?

She found it hard to believe that her friends, all more experienced than she was, had never felt this wrenching, ecstatic, frightening awareness that their world had tilted on its axis, and everything had been thrown out of perspective. Perhaps they had never really loved any of the men who had shared their beds.

It dawned on her that she had had a narrow escape from Michael. After all, they had grown up together, they liked each other enormously. How many people would have taken that last, inevitable step up the church aisle? Quite a few, she suspected. And if she had done that, she would never have known that this, this wonderful, awesome feeling, ever existed. She would have lived her life asleep.

Yes, she thought confusingly. I've been asleep. All my life I've been asleep, waiting for this one man to come along and wake me up.

It was an effort to force herself to think realistically about their relationship. *Her* life might have been overturned, but his had not. To him, she was a woman he had slept with, one he fancied, but beyond that there was nothing.

'You know what I mean,' he said, and she had to think a bit before she realised what he was talking about. 'Are you listening? You look as though you're a million miles away.'

I was, she thought sadly. Away on a wonderful planet somewhere, far removed from reality.

'Yes, I'm listening.'

'Well,' he drawled, gazing at her with those mesmerising eyes of his. 'Apart from vanishing off to our respective beds, I suggest we vanish off to somewhere altogether more distant. My offer still stands.' He absent-mindedly circled her nipple with his finger, smiling slightly as it eagerly responded to his touch.

'And so does my reply.' She sighed heavily and when she looked at him, his black brows had met in a frown.

'What do you mean?'

'I mean that I'm still not prepared to be your mistress.'

'We've just made love,' he said harshly. 'Why, if you had no intention of coming with me?'

'To satisfy my curiosity.'

'What?' he bellowed, sitting up. 'You used me to satisfy your curiosity?'

'Well, perhaps I didn't phrase that quite right...' She sat up and he moved away to stand with his back to her, his hands gripping the edge of the desk. She could see the muscles in his arms standing out, and she walked over to him, reaching out to touch him placatingly on his shoulder.

'Don't touch me!' he roared. He spun round to look at her, his face thunderous, and she shrank back a couple of steps. He moved forward, closing the space between them.

'You're coming to Italy with me,' he told her, and she shook her head. 'Oh, yes, my lovely, no more cosy Benjamin and Corinna twosome.'

'How can you say that?'

He looked away, then his eyes flicked back to hers. The tiger, she thought weakly, had been denied its meal, and it wasn't about to walk away without a fight. Standing there, naked, his hard body bronzed, he did look frighteningly untamed.

'You wouldn't want Benjamin to be disillusioned with you, would you?' There was a fierce, cruel twist to his mouth, and she folded her arms protectively across her breasts.

She should never have given in, but how could she explain that it was love and not lust that had made her do it?

'What do you mean?'

'How do you think he would feel if he knew that his golden girl slept with me, cold-bloodedly slept with me, *to satisfy her curiosity*? I don't think my father would be too impressed with a woman who's only interested in a man as a one-night stand, do you?'

'You can't be serious.'

'I am deadly serious.' They stared at each other in silence. He had struck at her most vulnerable point, Corinna realised. She loved Benjamin, he was the father she had been denied, and the thought of seeing him turn away from her in disappointment was unbearable.

'You're joking, Antonio, I know you are.' Her voice was hesitant though, and she looked at him wide-eyed.

'Watch me.'

Two words, but they were as convincing as if he had sat down and written a thesis on the seriousness of his intentions.

'My friends,' she tried feebly, 'my mother.'

'The postal system is very good and there'll be telephones.'

'I'll think about it.'

His hand snapped out, reaching to hold her neck in a threatening embrace. 'I want your answer now.'

Corinna looked down at her feet, and finally said, 'Then all right. You have what you want. Your plaything until you decide to discard me.'

His hand fell to his side and he looked away. 'Or until you decide to discard me,' he murmured in such a low voice that she barely caught the words. 'We'll play out this game of passion, Corinna Steadman,' he said savagely, 'and if you didn't want that, you should never have made love with me. Weren't you ever taught that if you play with fire, you might get burnt?'

The electric tension stretched like elastic between them, and at last she turned away and began pulling on her clothes. She couldn't look at him. She had not wanted to be his mistress, she hated him having blackmailed her into that situation, but something was pounding in her head, a strange, dizzy excitement at the thought that she could indulge her love just a little longer.

She left him standing by the window, staring out broodingly, and ran up to her bedroom.

Two hours later, lying in a bed which felt awfully cold without another warm body beside her, Corinna hugged her pillow to herself and tried to fall asleep.

It was useless. There was too much going on in her head for her even to shut her eyes. She had already had a long bath, tried to read a book, switched off the bedside light then switched it back on, tried to write a letter. But she couldn't concentrate on anything. There was so much to think about. She would have to tell her mother, Michael, Benjamin, her friends. The list was endless.

She was on a crazy rollercoaster ride and she didn't want to think what would happen when the time came for her to step off.

How was she to know that by the following evening that rollercoaster would come crashing down around her?

# CHAPTER NINE

In the end, Corinna only managed to get to sleep as the new day was stirring from behind the veil of night. But when she did finally fall asleep, she slept surprisingly well. And she had no idea how long she would have continued sleeping if she hadn't been awakened by a knocking on the bedroom door.

Then she struggled up and, as she did so, everything that had happened the night before came rushing back into her head, in a great tidal wave of panicky confusion. She, whose ventures beyond English soil had been few and far between, was going to Italy. She should, she knew, be frightened, resentful, apprehensive. And she was, but she was also darkly and disturbingly excited. How, she thought, could a grey-eyed kidnapper rouse this bitter thrill? But she knew the answer. Demeaning or not, wasn't her craving for him so uncontrollable, like a flame that had become a raging bushfire, that she was prepared to follow him to the ends of the earth? And let common sense go knocking on someone else's door?

All these things flashed in and out of her head with bewildering speed in the time it took her to open the bedroom door.

She had noticed, when she opened her eyes, that it was already nearly lunchtime. She couldn't possibly remain in bed any longer, anyway.

It was something of a shock to see Maria standing outside her bedroom door. Her eyes were pink. She looked as though she had been crying.

'May I come in? Please?' she asked, dabbing her eyes with a little lace handkerchief, and Corinna nodded without saying anything.

'I am so sorry to intrude on you like this,' Maria said, turning around. 'You were asleep. I had no idea.'

'It doesn't matter,' Corinna said quickly. 'It's late. I was going to get up anyway.' She yawned and gave Maria an apologetic smile.

The other woman was obviously dressed for her trip back to Italy. She was wearing a pair of gold and black leggings, the first Corinna had seen her in since she arrived at Deanbridge House, a black cotton short-sleeved jumper, which repeated the gold pattern on the leggings, and a pair of flat shoes. She looked elegantly comfortable.

Corinna pulled her bathrobe around her and beckoned to Maria to sit down, at which point Maria's lips trembled and Corinna had a sneaking suspicion that she was about to witness an onslaught of tears.

'Whatever is the matter?' she asked, concerned. This was so unlike the controlled Maria which had been much in evidence since she had arrived that Corinna was almost tempted to send for the doctor.

'I——' Maria took a deep breath, which seemed to steady her, '—I thought that I would come to see you because...' The threat of tears hovered close by once again. 'You are so very kind. Forgiving me my unforgivable behaviour. You have acted so—what is the word?—decently. Now, here I am, bringing you this news. No.' She stood up and began to walk towards the door. 'I cannot be so cruel. I will not be so cruel.'

Corinna stopped her in her tracks and said, alarmed, 'What are you talking about?'

There was hesitation in those luminous dark eyes as they looked at her, then Maria sighed and sank gracefully on to one of the chairs in the room.

'I know you will hate me for this,' she said, pausing to consider how best to continue, 'and I thought about it long and hard, and...' She lifted her eyes to Corinna and chewed her lip nervously. Corinna had the insane desire to feel her forehead for fever, just in case Maria was hallucinating. She certainly was behaving very strangely.

'Just tell me,' Corinna said quietly. 'What could have upset you like this?' She swept her hair away from her face and sat on the edge of the bed, so that they were opposite each other.

'I overheard Antonio and his father talking,' Maria said in a low voice, and Corinna knew, uneasily, that what was coming was not going to be good. 'Shall I continue?' Maria asked, reading her expression, and Corinna nodded.

'You will not like it.' The other woman drew a deep breath and shuddered slightly. 'They were in the study,' Maria murmured, and Corinna had to lean forward to hear her. 'This morning. Early. The door was half open and I would have entered, I was about to knock, but then I heard them mention your name and something stopped me, I don't know what.' Her black eyes begged forgiveness.

'What did you hear?' Corinna asked, and her mouth felt as though it was stuffed with cotton wool.

'Benjamin. He was talking to Antonio about that holiday you requested. You remember?'

Corinna nodded.

'Then he said, in an odd, tired voice, that he did not know what to do about you.' Maria's elegant fingers twisted and curled around the lace handkerchief. 'Are you quite sure you want me to continue?'

Corinna nodded once more. The colour had drained from her face and she felt as though she was dreaming, caught up in some frightful nightmare. It was like walking towards something that was desperately frightening, but you couldn't stop, your feet were propelling you onwards, even though you badly wanted to turn tail and run.

'He said,' Maria continued in the same slow, agonised voice, 'that he no longer needed you, but he did not have the heart to tell you so. He was back on his feet, he said, he no longer needed a caretaker. I would have left at the point. Already I had heard too much, but then Antonio spoke. He laughed a bit, then he said that that was no problem. That you would be leaving with him to go to Italy. He said it would only last a few weeks, three months at the most, but that that would give Benjamin enough time to get his thoughts together and write you a letter telling you not to return to Deanbridge House.'

There was a little old-fashioned clock on the dressing-table. Now, the only sound in the room was the ticking of that clock.

'Are you sure?' Corinna asked, in a small, dazed voice and Maria nodded with hollow-eyed sadness.

'*Has* Antonio asked you to go to Italy with him?' she asked and Corinna nodded, looking away. Her eyes felt like pools of unshed tears and she found that she was gripping the edge of the bed tightly, so tightly that her knuckles were white.

'I am so sorry,' Maria said, glancing down. She had an ornate ring on one of her fingers, and she fiddled with it, tugging it up and down. 'I wish I could say that my ears were playing the tricks on me, but I heard them, as clearly as I hear you now. Antonio was laughing a little when he said about you going to Italy.'

'Did he say anything else?' Corinna whispered, and Maria hesitated, then said with a rush, 'He said he surprised himself with this sudden appetite for a blonde, gauche girl, but that it would do you good anyway. Then he shut the door. I nearly jumped out of my skin. I thought that they would find me outside, eavesdropping so to speak, even though I did not intend it that way.'

Corinna stared in front of her, not saying anything and not seeing anything. It all made sense. Maria couldn't possibly have known that she and Antonio had been planning on going to Italy. The woman was not telepathic. She closed her eyes and saw Antonio in her mind, wearing a mocking, derogatory smile on his face as he told Benjamin that their affair wouldn't last three months. What else had he said behind that closed door? It crossed her mind that there was something a little odd about such a scene taking place, but it was only a fleeting consideration because how else could Maria have known about Italy? And why would she fabricate such a story when she had already accepted the fact that Antonio was not interested in her?

As for Benjamin, it was true that he no longer needed her the way that he once had. She had fulfilled a role of companion before his son had arrived. Now he no longer needed such a companion. He had the challenge of his new job, a feeling perhaps of long overdue independence. Did he really want her tagging along behind him? Holding his hand and reminding him to take his pills?

'I shall have to leave,' she said, standing up and restlessly prowling the room. 'At once.'

Maria didn't say anything, but her silence spoke of her agreement, and with a sudden need for someone to share her agitated, urgent desire to leave, Corinna said in a strained voice, 'What shall I do? I shall have to see Benjamin before I leave. He deserves at least that.' She made no mention of Antonio. She had been desperate to know what it would be like to make love with him, she had ignored the little voice that pleaded caution; what else could she expect? Humiliation was her reward, and she would just have to swallow it, even if it was like broken glass in her throat.

'I am not sure,' Maria murmured, and Corinna looked at the other woman in surprise.

'But I've been with him for a while. He's my friend.'

'Which is why perhaps you shouldn't confront him with a decision to leave. Do you not see? It would stir his guilt.'

Corinna frowned. She couldn't seem to think straight. Did that make sense? It appeared to, in a weird kind of way.

'Perhaps a letter,' Maria suggested softly. 'Tell him that you have to go immediately. Something perhaps to do with a relative? Or a friend? There is no need to be specific. But you can say that you will be in touch very soon, to talk to him face to face. He is out of the house with Antonio at the moment. They are both at the office, setting up the computer systems and getting the last things sorted out.'

'You think I should run?' Corinna asked doubtfully. She wasn't about to follow anyone's advice, but it was oddly reassuring to be discussing this with someone else, especially when her brain felt like cotton wool.

Maria shrugged and looked at her watch. 'My God! The time! I have a taxi booked to take me to the airport. I must go. It comes soon, in five minutes.' She stood up and clasped Corinna by the hand. 'Whatever you do, good luck.' Then she was gone, leaving the air smelling of some fragrant perfume.

A deathly numbness settled over her. She had no idea what to do and she couldn't seem to rouse herself even to think of anything. Eventually, she began packing her suitcases. They had been stuffed into the wardrobe ever since she had arrived and they smelled faintly stale, but she didn't even notice that as she flung clothes into them, crushing them down, cramming all sorts of things in between, not caring that when they were next yanked open they would spill out crumpled clothing that needed ironing.

A letter. Perhaps Maria was right. She sat down once she had finished packing and wrote several versions of a note, discarding them all, until, through sheer exhaustion, she briefly explained that she had to leave, an emergency at home, that she would be in touch. Then she called a taxi and waited. Every five minutes she looked anxiously at her watch. What if Antonio walked through the front door before she had left? She didn't think that she could bear it. She wouldn't know what to say.

It seemed like ages before she heard the rapping on the front door, then she quickly dashed to open it, hustling the bemused taxi driver along with her cases as if the hounds of hell were on her tail, and only just remembering to stick the note for Benjamin on the little circular table at the foot of the staircase.

As the taxi pulled out of the long drive that led away from Deanbridge House, she closed her eyes and felt some tears trickle down her cheeks. So many months of happiness and now this desperate flight. She would call Benjamin as soon as she settled back into some kind of routine. Perhaps visit him. Explain as much as she possibly could. She would keep in touch with him because she couldn't bear the thought of never seeing him again.

Part of her mind rose up with images of Antonio and she relentlessly repelled these with the best weapon she had to hand: bitterness. She tried to close her mind off completely to the memory of their lovemaking and she succeeded in so far as she eventually fell asleep in the back of the taxi, only waking up when the car had pulled to a stop outside her mother's house.

Now, Corinna thought wearily, the nightmare continues. She paid the taxi driver, who looked at her curiously, having noticed, no doubt, she thought, the many copious tears shed between Deanbridge House and here.

She had underestimated the amount of explanation which, over the next two weeks, were to prove necessary to her mother, her friends, everyone, it seemed, including the dustbin man. They all wanted to know what had made her leave her job and every single time Corinna opened her mouth with her rehearsed story about Benjamin being back on his feet, about needing a change of environment, about a sudden restlessness that had overtaken her, she could hear her words ringing feebly in her ears.

Her mother was the most difficult to evade. 'It's a man, isn't it?' she had asked immediately, her mouth sharply disapproving. 'I hope you haven't got yourself pregnant, my girl. You should have married young Michael, you should have settled down with a reliable boy instead of throwing up everything and taking some job in the middle of nowhere.' She followed her around the house, her eyes narrowed, yapping at her heels until Corinna wanted to scream.

She closed her ears, and kept up the same refrain in her head. It was all for the best. It would never have worked out with Antonio. She would have retreated from Italy, wounded and hurt, and with even more explanations to try and think of. And anyway, wasn't it nice being back home? She was seeing a lot more of her friends, wasn't she? And things would be better when she got another job at one of the hospitals, perhaps the one she had left, and could find somewhere in the nurses' lodgings. Then at least she wouldn't have to live with her mother's tight-faced curiosity all the time.

Underneath the veneer, though, she was plagued by memories of Antonio. She saw him in every stranger's back, heard his voice across crowded rooms in pubs, then a strangling excitement would claw at her stomach, only to fade away as soon as she realised her mistake. She couldn't get him out of her mind.

There was some comfort to be had from her friends, who rallied around her with unquestioning support. They all had their own busy lives to lead, and they had accepted her explanations about deciding to return to London without a great deal of doubt. They had never really understood her reasons for leaving in the first place. It seemed quite natural that she should return.

When, after three and a half weeks, a post came up at the teaching hospital where she used to work, Corinna accepted. Antonio might be as vivid in her mind as though it had only been yesterday that she had looked into his eyes, but Deanbridge House was slowly fading into the background. The memories of the pleasure she had derived from the long, peaceful days there were becoming dimmer and more intangible.

She still hadn't got around to telephoning Benjamin. Several times she had her hand on the receiver, and then something would make her withdraw. Perhaps it was the thought that hearing his voice down the line would be too heartbreaking. She would remember too much.

I still need a little more time, she thought, to find myself. When I'm more settled I'll call him, visit perhaps.

She was returning home one afternoon, walking slowly up the street to her house, her mind preoccupied with the usual disturbing memories which seemed to have become part and parcel of her daily existence, when she saw her mother at the door, with her hands on her hips, and an even more ominous expression on her face than usual.

Corinna waved with an inward sigh. Mother, she thought, I do love you, but sometimes you just make it so damned difficult. As she drew closer, she felt an uneasy gnawing in the pit of her stomach, the sort of feeling you got when the telephone rang at three in the morning, or a telegram unexpectedly got delivered, or the boss called you into his office *for a little chat*. Some things did not herald good news.

Corinna was breathless by the time she had run up the street to the door.

'What's the matter?' she asked, looking worried. 'What is it?'

'You have a visitor,' her mother said flatly.

'Oh, is that all?' Corinna stepped past her mother, chatting to her over her shoulder while she removed her jacket and slung it on the coat stand in the small hallway. Summer had abruptly died a death. The warm breezes which she could remember at Deanbridge House had given way, without warning, to a sharp, unseasonable cold. The weather men had half-heartedly mentioned the possibility of an Indian summer, but such references were becoming fewer and more far between. Soon it would be winter, with short, chilly days and early nights, settling over London like a thick, black blanket. She had always found winter depressing. It made her lethargic, unwilling to do much. She wasn't looking forward to shifts at the hospital, travelling back in the darkness on the London underground.

'I can't believe I'm going to be getting up at six o'clock in the morning from next Monday,' she was saying, while her mother followed in her wake. 'Look at this weather! It's freezing out there.'

Then she stopped and stared into the small lounge with her mouth half open. Had she just been talking about the weather? She didn't remember. Her feet had become lead and the blood had rushed to her head with a suddenness that left her feeling dizzy.

'I'll leave you two alone, shall I?' her mother asked from behind her, her voice brimming with curiosity, and Corinna turned around, thinking, No! Don't do that! Please don't do that! But the words, clear as a bell in her head, didn't manage to make it to her mouth, and she was left with the door firmly closed behind her.

'Hello.' It seemed an utterly inappropriate greeting to the man who had been on her mind ever since she had left Deanbridge House. She took a few steps forward, feeling as though she was on the brink of teetering over. 'What are you doing here?'

Antonio was looking at her expressionlessly. His arms were resting lightly on the sides of his chair and his legs were crossed. He looked indolently, horribly, awesomely handsome. Had she forgotten how good-looking he was? She hadn't thought so but she must have done because she felt shock-waves tearing through her at the sight of him.

'How long have you been here?' she asked weakly, sitting down and leaning forward slightly. She was wearing a pair of jeans and a baggy jumper, and she tucked her feet under the chair.

'Half an hour maybe.' There was no smile on that face. He looked cold, remote and a little bit bored. 'Your mother was kind enough to give me some tea and biscuits.'

'What are you doing here?' she repeated her original question, and he stood up and began to prowl restlessly around the room. It was not a large lounge. There was their faded apricot and green flowered three-piece suite, a television on a stand in one corner, an occasional table with a pretty lamp on it and a few porcelain ornaments, a few other bits and pieces. Ever since her father had deserted them, money had been tight, a fact which her mother had never let her forget, and now it seemed shabby and small. Antonio dwarfed it. She half expected him to knock something over, but he was a graceful mover.

'My father is ill,' he said abruptly, and she half stood with a look of horror on her face.

'How ill? What's wrong with him? Has he called the doctor out?'

'My, my, my,' Antonio said sarcastically, 'such tender concern. If I didn't know better I would have said that you actually cared one way or the other.'

'I do!'

'So much that you left Deanbridge House without even telling the old man goodbye?' His face was flushed with anger. It slipped out from behind the mask of indifference and surprised her. She would have expected him to be annoyed with her. She had left without saying goodbye to Benjamin, and she had also run out on Antonio. That must have hurt his pride. But the depth of his anger seemed to go beyond that.

'I explained why I had to leave,' she mumbled, confused and dismayed.

'Oh, of course you did. Unexpected circumstances. How revealing. I don't suppose it even crossed your mind that he might have been worried about you?'

No, it hadn't really crossed her mind. After all, hadn't he said to Antonio that he no longer needed her? She had taken the uncomfortable decision out of his hands and she thought, maybe a little misguidedly, that he might have been a touch relieved.

'I'm sorry.' It sounded inadequate, but dammit, why did she have to sit here as though she had committed some kind of crime!

'Well, I don't give a damn about your sorrow,' Antonio said harshly. 'It sounds a little hollow to my ears. But my father asked me to come here and fetch you, and fetch you I shall.'

She couldn't disguise the look of sudden panic that flashed across her features, and he said, moving towards her, with a snarl in his voice, 'Clearly you don't relish the prospect of seeing him again. Believe me, this is the last place I want to be, but I'm reluctantly obeying orders. He's taken to bed and he won't budge until you're there, so come on.'

'I can't just leave!'

'No? I assure you that's just what you're going to do. You can tell your unexpected circumstance that he'll have to take a back seat for a few days.'

'What?' Now she was thoroughly confused, but she didn't have time to dwell on what he had said, because he had gripped her arm and was propelling her towards the door.

'You can't just stroll in here and order me about! This is my house! Well, my mother's house.'

'I will give you five minutes to pack your bag, and if you're not down, I shall come and do it for you.'

'Who do you think you are?' Corinna asked angrily.

Antonio looked at his watch. 'Now,' he said coldly. 'I have already wasted the better part of my day running this ridiculous errand. I don't intend to waste any more.'

She felt the prick of tears behind her eyes. Ridiculous errand? Is that what I am?

'Poor you,' she said with equal coldness. 'I'm so sorry that you had to put yourself out.'

'So am I.'

She turned away and left the room to find her mother standing in the hall, hovering, and Corinna sighed wearily.

'Benjamin's ill,' she said. 'I'm going to have to return to Deanbridge House, probably just for one night.'

She began walking up the stairs, and her mother followed.

'Who is that man?'

'His son.'

'You never mentioned him.'

'Mother,' she said, beginning to toss some clothes into a bag, 'I didn't think you would be very interested.'

'So I'm an unfit mother, is that it? I brought you up single-handedly, and now all you can tell me is that I'm an unfit mother.'

'No,' Corinna said, turning to face her, 'it's just that...'

Her mother looked down awkwardly. 'Are you in love with that man?'

'What makes you say that?'

'The look on your face.'

They stared at each other and a rare thread of understanding passed between them.

'Yes, I am,' Corinna said simply. 'More fool me.'

'I should have admitted this sooner,' her mother said. 'I made mistakes with your father. Be careful.'

Corinna nodded. This was a conversation which would have to be resumed. Right now, she would have to fly because she wouldn't put it past Antonio Silver to stride into her bedroom and drag her out.

He was waiting impatiently for her at the bottom of the stairs and she did her utmost to ignore his presence completely. She didn't want to see that contemptuous sneer on his face, or hear about how many better things he had to do.

They drove through London in an atmosphere of uncomfortable silence. He didn't have anything to say to her and he was making no effort to be polite. As far as he was concerned, he had been sent on a mission and had begrudgingly completed it. Conversation was a fringe benefit with which he was not prepared to indulge her. It was incredible to think that this was the same man who had made love to her, had sent her soaring to some planet far above the stars.

After nearly an hour of silence, she took a deep breath and said a little desperately, 'I know you must be angry with me. I left without saying a word to your father, or to you either. I just want you to know——'

She didn't have the opportunity to complete the sentence. He banged his fist against the steering-wheel with such controlled fury that she recoiled in fear.

'I didn't ask for explanations, and I don't want them,' he bit out, his eyes fixed on the road, and she stared at the hard profile with a mixture of alarm and bewilderment. Again she got the feeling that something, somewhere, wasn't quite right. It was no more than an intangible suspicion floating somewhere at the back of her mind, and she frowned for a bit, then lapsed back into silence, staring through the window, angry at him, at herself, at the world.

She didn't for one moment think that he was angry because her abrupt departure had hurt him. How could he be seriously hurt when he had only planned on their relationship lasting a couple of months, until his appetite for her had been satisfied? No, she had wounded his pride, that was it. He had been so sure that he had the bowl of cream within his grasp and, just as he was about to lower his head and have a drink, it had been pulled away from him. That was what lay behind his anger. That and the thought that she had abandoned his father. Not that he could talk, she thought, clinging to this to overcome the seeds of guilt that she had felt ever since she had left Deanbridge House. Hadn't he abandoned Benjamin even more callously than she had done? She half hoped that he would raise the matter with her once more, so that she could lay all that at his door, but he didn't. They completed the journey in silence and, as soon as the car had stopped, he got out and walked up to the front door, not bothering to open hers and ignoring her case which had been lying on the back seat. I didn't want to fetch you, his attitude said, I don't want you here, and the less I have to do with you the better.

She felt utterly miserable as she followed him into the hall, lugging her case with her.

He turned to look at her with steely eyes and said in a hard voice, 'He's upstairs in his bedroom. I won't bother to show you up.'

'Of course not,' she said, meeting his eyes, 'why should you? You have far more important things to do, I'm sure. You've made that quite clear on the drive up.'

'Did you expect conversation?' His voice was cold. 'Some light-hearted banter, perhaps?'

'Politeness would have been enough.'

'I don't feel very polite towards you.' He had his hands thrust into his pockets and she could see that they were balled into fists.

There was no response to that and he expected none. He turned on his heel, and she looked at him as he walked off in the direction of the study, then she ran up the stairs, arriving at Benjamin's room breathless and red-faced.

Now that she was here, she didn't know what she was going to say. How ill exactly was he? Antonio had been uncommunicative on the subject, only informing her that he had retreated to bed. She knocked and then pushed open the door to find Benjamin on the bed with the covers pulled up to his chin, but his eyes were as bright and shrewd as ever, although he lowered them mournfully as she walked into the bedroom and perched awkwardly on the edge of the bed.

'Benjamin,' she began, 'I'm sorry I walked out on you like that. I really am. I've been meaning to phone...' Her voice trailed off with the inadequacy of the words. Meaning to phone—it was along the same lines as telling someone that their cheque was in the post.

He sighed, a small disappointed sound, and Corinna could feel her face becoming red and flushed under his scrutiny.

'It's good to see you, girl,' he said. His voice sounded weak.

'And you,' she murmured with sincerity. 'I wouldn't have left, but...'

'Exceptional circumstances. Yes.' Another sigh. 'I hope they've been resolved? What were they anyway?' He coughed and shut his eyes, reopening them very quickly, though, to gauge her reaction.

'I can't explain, Benjamin. They're very private.'

'Of course.' There was a little silence. 'Not that you're under any obligation to explain.' He coughed again. 'After all, I'm only an old man and you were only the ray of sunshine in my miserable existence.'

That sounded very dramatic to her, and she looked to see if there was laughter anywhere on his face, but he was looking at her seriously, if a little coyly.

'No,' Corinna felt obliged to expand, 'actually, something happened; I had to leave.'

'Yes?'

'What's the matter with you, Benjamin? Antonio didn't say. What sort of relapse have you had? Have you called out the doctor?'

'That quack? Over my dead body.'

'I keep telling you, he's very good in his field.' This was beginning to sound like a re-run of one of their past conversations. 'You can't just take to bed. Tell me your symptoms.'

'Depression,' he said in a faint, weak voice. 'That's my symptom. Depression. And I don't need that quack to come here and fill me up with any more pills.' He reached out for her hand and she slipped hers into his. 'This house has been miserable since you left.'

Corinna smiled. 'I'm sure you're exaggerating,' she said, and she couldn't prevent a little dryness from creeping into her voice.

'Oh, no. For instance, Edna's been terrible. Moody and trying to force me out of bed.' Loosely translated, Corinna read this to mean that Edna had tried to open the curtains and get him at least to get some fresh air on his face. 'It must be the menopause,' he added tartly, and she grinned.

'I think Edna saw the back of that some time ago.'

'Pah! Then there's Antonio.' He looked at her from under lowered eyelids. 'He hasn't been himself these past few weeks.'

'No?' Her voice had dropped a few degrees. She didn't want to get into a discussion about his son and, anyway, she didn't see what he had to do with it at all.

'No. After you left, I persuaded him to stay a little longer, but he's done nothing but storm around. Not at all soothing for an old man like me. We both know about my blood-pressure, don't we?'

She nodded.

'Which,' he continued weakly, 'is why I would like to see you two make up. Because I might be old but I'm no fool. Whatever happened between you and I have no idea what it is, it's thrown Antonio's nose out of joint. And you too, I'm sure. And I'd really like to see the two most important people in my life make up their differences. Before the grim reaper comes.' This last bit was definitely very theatrical and he must have sensed that because he cleared his throat loudly and looked a bit sheepish. 'Go and fetch him,' he said. 'Bring him here and make an old man happy.'

Corinna listened to his speech with growing alarm, and at the end of it she stammered off a stream of excuses, tried to tell him that he was mistaken, but he had sunk into silence and in the end she had no option but to leave the bedroom and head for the study, and the one person she didn't want to see.

# CHAPTER TEN

ANTONIO wasn't working. He was standing with his back to the door, staring out of the window. Corinna looked at the erect, lean-hipped body through the open door and took a deep breath. Even from this angle, it was easy to see that he was in a foul temper. It was apparent in the way he held himself, like someone who would rather be doing something altogether more violent than contemplating the scenery.

She knocked half-heartedly on the door, even though it was open, and she saw him stiffen. How encouraging, she thought glumly. This is like walking into a lion's den, and a hungry lion at that. He didn't want to have anything to do with her, and he was not a man to go through the motions of courtesy. Did he think that it was any easier for her? At most all he was suffering was a blow to his masculine pride. Pride, on the other hand, was the least of her worries.

'I—Benjamin sent me...' she stammered nervously, and he turned slowly to face her. Very slowly. The grey eyes skirted over her coldly and returned to her face.

'What for?' It was an indifferent question, which didn't make it any easier for her to continue, and this began to make her angry. She didn't want to be here, like some fifteen-year-old schoolgirl in the headmaster's office, and she resented it.

'Look,' she said with equal coldness, 'I don't want to be here any more than you want me to be here, but Benjamin's sent me and there was nothing I could do.'

175

'So what does he want?' Antonio asked, bored.

'He seems to think that there's some friction between us...'

'Docs he? How astute.'

'And,' she continued, with what she considered monumental patience, 'he wants us to heal the rift.'

'Does he, now?' Antonio smiled coldly. 'I can't imagine why.'

'Stop making this difficult for me,' Corinna said with a sigh, and his brows met in a furious frown.

'And stop acting like a victim,' he snarled by way of response, 'it just doesn't wash with me.' He looked as though he was about to expand on this, but he didn't. Instead he turned away, his jaw hard. 'Oh, for God's sake,' he said finally, 'I suppose there's no use standing here and debating the issue. He wants rifts to be healed; well, why don't we oblige?' He gave her another one of those cold, vaguely cruel smiles. 'Or at least give the appearance of doing so.'

He nodded in the direction of the door and Corinna spun round, walking quickly along the corridor and up the staircase, uncomfortably aware of Antonio's silent, long-limbed tread behind her.

In the time she had been away from Deanbridge House, she had played and replayed a thousand imaginary scenarios between herself and Antonio, and none of them was remotely like this. This was more awful than she had ever thought possible. She had expected his anger, but not the relentless, unforgiving depth of it. The only thing which she had correctly gauged was her own miserable, yearning reaction to him. Oh, that was spot-on, she thought unhappily.

They arrived outside Benjamin's bedroom, and Antonio leant forward to whisper in her ear, 'Don't forget, darling, to make it convincing because I have no intention of repeating the exercise. Not that that should be difficult for you. You specialise in hypocrisy, don't you? You're a two-faced bitch *par excellence* and, take it from me, I've seen quite a few.'

'I'm sure you have,' Corinna said sweetly, even though she felt as though she had been sliced open with a very sharp knife. 'You know what they say about birds of a feather.' She caught enough of his reaction to that before she turned away, and it was not pleasant. He looked as though he wanted to hit her. She knocked, pushed open the door and plastered a smile on her face.

Benjamin was sitting up with an expectant expression on his face.

'At last,' he said, in what sounded suspiciously like a satisfied voice. 'I thought you'd run off again.'

'You're looking much better, Father,' Antonio said, moving to stand next to Corinna, and Benjamin nodded.

'Amazing what a pretty face will do,' he said smugly, 'isn't it, son?'

'Oh, yes,' Antonio said softly, 'amazing.' This was directed at her, she knew. Amazing, he implied, and not very pleasant either. 'I hate to disappoint you, though,' he said, 'but there's no rift between us so this little joint exercise is all a bit futile and pointless.'

'Humour an old man,' Benjamin replied. 'An old, sick man.'

'Fine. What would you like us to do?'

There was a little silence while Benjamin digested this, then he said weakly, 'I know you've said this is pointless, but I can't help sensing some animosity between you. I thought you two were getting along just fine, and then my dear nurse departs and you spend weeks storming through here and frightening us all. Naturally I put two and two together. What can you expect?'

Corinna smiled weakly, feeling faint, and Antonio said, with a hint of impatience in his voice, 'All right. We'll humour you, if that's what you want.' He turned to her and she felt the force of his personality washing over her like a blast of cold wind. 'Corinna, smile and tell my father that he's been imagining things.'

She smiled and told him, and Benjamin said with a cough, 'I'm so glad. I just want you two to kiss and make up. It would make me so happy.'

She felt her stomach constrict. This wasn't what she had expected. She didn't want Antonio near her. Least of all, she didn't want him to kiss her.

'Please,' Benjamin murmured in a feeble voice which she impotently suspected was manufactured for the purpose.

Antonio shrugged and turned to her and she felt a film of fine perspiration break out over her body. He wasn't going to do this, was he? But he was. He held her arm and lowered his head, placing his cool lips over hers. It was a brief, momentary contact to which she didn't even respond, but she felt as though every part of her had been intimately touched. Her body was suddenly fired with a craving which left her breathless and she took a couple of steps backwards.

'Thank you,' Benjamin was saying in the same feeble voice. 'I'm so glad this has all been sorted out.' He closed his eyes and lay back on the pillow, and she heard herself ask, 'Is it all right if I go to my room now? I'd like to unpack and have a bath...'

Her voice sounded as if it was coming from a long way off. There had been no emotion in Antonio's kiss. He might have been kissing a stranger, or some inanimate object in the room, but it still left her giddy and disorientated and she wanted to burst into tears. Was it always going to be like this? Would her body forever crave him, so that all relationships with men became spoilt through comparison?

She walked towards the door on unsteady legs and was hurrying back to her bedroom, unaware of Antonio behind her until she felt him gripping her arms, propelling her into her room, slamming the door behind her.

'Please,' she said, panic-stricken, 'what are you doing? Please leave!'

'Oh, no,' he murmured softly, with intent in his eyes, 'I didn't think that kiss was at all convincing, did you? Not compared with some of the others we've exchanged.' He curled his fingers into her hair and before she could protest, his mouth hit hers and she felt the anger spilling out of him like poison.

He kissed her hard, mercilessly, forcing her lips open and then thrusting his tongue inside the warm wetness of her mouth.

Corinna ineffectually tried to push him away but that only invoked a stronger reaction.

'I could kill you,' he muttered savagely, pushing her on to the bed, and then standing in front of her, raking his fingers through his hair.

'Why?'

'You lied to me,' he said, 'you damn well lied to me!'

'I didn't! I don't know what you're talking about.'

'Spin me another one, Corinna. You left that boyfriend of yours, *you said*? You weren't suited, *you said*? Was the prospect of Italy with me so terrifying that you decided to retreat to what you knew, even if you didn't much like it?' he jeered. 'Is that it? You decided that a safe little life with your safe little boyfriend was what you wanted after all?'

'What?' Her eyes were round with bewilderment. She had no idea what he was talking about. He had suddenly veered off track, leaving her on some unknown road miles behind. 'You're mad.'

'Don't give me that innocent look!' he roared. He reached into his pocket and his hand whipped out with frightening speed. For a split second she thought that he was going to strike her, but he didn't. He had thrown something down on the bed. A piece of paper, and she stared at it as if it was going to rear up and attack her at any minute.

'What is it?' she asked in a small voice, and he laughed. It was a nasty sound.

'Really. Read it. I'm sure your memory will come flooding back to you.'

Corinna picked up the piece of paper with trembling fingers and read.

Dear Antonio

I don't know how to say this but I won't be coming with you after all. I've changed my mind, you see, a woman's prerogative. Italy with you sounded very exciting, and I admit that I was tempted, but thankfully I was not so stupid. I had a call from Michael. Do you remember I told you about him? He is very ill, he has been in an accident, and this has made me realise that I would be a fool not to marry him. I prefer a lifetime of security and contentment to three months of fun. Sorry. Corinna.

She put the paper back on the bed, folding it very neatly because that gave her something to do with her hands.

'Still suffering from amnesia, darling?'

'Where did you get this?'

'Where you left it. Slipped under my bedroom door.'

'I didn't put it there.'

'No? Sudden gust of wind did it for you?' His voice was derisive.

'You're crazy.'

'To have ever believed you to be anything other than a lying cheat, yes.' There was raw fury in his voice even though he sounded quite controlled and civilised.

'I didn't write this.' Her mind felt like a computer which had been overloaded and was on the point of shutting down. Where did that letter come from? What the hell was going on? 'It's not my writing,' she continued, 'it's not my signature. Someone's tried to make it look like mine, but it isn't.'

'And pigs fly.'

'It's the truth!' Her eyes flashed angrily. 'I'm not asking you to believe me, but it happens to be the truth. I never wrote that! I wouldn't!'

'No?'

'No!' They looked at each other, and she realised that she badly wanted to touch him.

'Then who did?' He still sounded cynical but there was hesitation in his voice now. 'Why did you leave? What made you do it?' She could still see the battle being fought in him between pride and a need to know, and she slowly explained everything. Maria, her change of attitude, that visit to her bedroom the morning after she and Antonio had made love, and with every word his face became more thunderous.

He sat on the bed, his features rigid.

'Why didn't you confront Benjamin? Why leave a note?'

'Maria...' Her voice faded into comprehending silence. 'Maria wrote that letter, didn't she?' Corinna asked. 'How did she know about Michael?'

'Answer me!'

She frowned and thought back, trying to retrace the conversation which now seemed like years ago. 'I was going to,' she said slowly, 'when Maria told me what she had overheard, I was going to wait and have a talk to him, but...'

'But she persuaded you that that wasn't such a good idea, and you believed her.'

'Yes,' Corinna admitted faintly. 'She said that that would put him in an awkward position, that he'd be forced to keep me on through some sense of duty. I believed her. You see, she'd been so nice the evening before, I...'

'You played into her hands.' He sat heavily on the bed, not looking at her but into the distance, thinking, then he said carefully, 'And so did I. She found out about that boyfriend of yours from me. Shortly after she arrived, she asked me about you, whether you didn't have some boyfriend tucked away somewhere. I flew into a rage. The thought was so distasteful that I told her that you had had a boyfriend by the name of Michael, but that that was history. I didn't understand how crazy I could feel just at the thought of you and a man, but I did. Afterwards, I forgot all about that conversation. She didn't.' He sighed and pressed his thumbs against his eyes. 'I always knew that she was manipulative, but not to what extent. She wanted me, and when I rejected her she reacted with the rage of a woman scorned. You see, Maria is an only child, born late to parents who had desperately been trying for years. She led a spoiled, pampered existence. Then she was sent abroad to study, and for the first time I think she realised that her innate intelligence was a far more powerful weapon than her looks and money. She returned to Italy to run her father's company, and she ran it with a rod of iron because she enjoyed power, she enjoyed having the ability to hire and fire. I never guessed how far she would go to make sure that you vanished from the scene, and I should have. On the day before she was due to fly, she came to me with a final plea for us to reconcile, and I told her that it was out of the question, that I was going to ask you to come back with me to Italy, and I guess that was when she hatched her little plot. First she wooed you with an apology, I suppose, then she went for the kill on the morning of her flight. She never overheard anything between my father and myself because there was nothing to overhear. How could you think that I would say anything like that to my father? He would have murdered me on the spot.'

'I was confused. I wasn't thinking straight.' It's a problem, she added to herself, that I seem to have recently developed. 'But how did she know that I'd do what I did?'

'She didn't. She just sowed her seeds and left the rest to Fate.'

Corinna nodded, speechless. Such malevolence was beyond her comprehension. 'I suppose she wrote that note to you...'

'Knowing I'd fall for it hook, line and sinker, because...'

'Because what?'

'Because——' he fixed his eyes on her face '—you were my weak spot. My Achilles' heel, and that's something I've never had to contend with in my life before.'

Her heart skipped a beat and began to race.

'I saw red. You and that man. You said you'd been involved. It never occurred to me that I had anything to fear from the past. Roberto, maybe. He was the present. But not some damn ex-boyfriend. I felt as though I'd been punched in the stomach. Worse. I couldn't even rustle up my pride, and pride was something I'd spent years perfecting. Pride was what kept me away from here. All the misunderstandings between my father and myself grew into unsurpassable mountains because of damn pride. But all I felt when I thought of you in another man's arms was blind rage. Blind, jealous rage, like a volcano.'

Now her racing heart was doing somersaults.

'Did you see him?' he asked suddenly.

'No,' Corinna said. 'Michael and I are finished. We were finished a long time ago, before I even came here to work for your father.'

There was a thick silence, then Antonio said, 'I don't suppose there's much point in...' He searched around for the right words and abandoned the attempt.

'Did you miss me?' Four words, one simple question, but she found that her body was rigid with tension.

'I...' He went a dark red. 'Yes. You—I—yes, I did. I couldn't get you out of my head. I felt I was losing my mind. I was due to return to Italy, but I couldn't. I found I was glued to these shores like an idiot who's fixated with being in the same country, at least, as his lover. God, I hated you.'

There wasn't hate in his eyes as they bored into hers. There was a passion which went to her head like incense.

'She played us for fools,' he said huskily, 'and if I ever get my hands on her, I'll teach her a lesson she won't forget in a hurry.' He stopped, then asked quickly, thickly, 'And you. Did you miss me? Did you?'

'Oh God,' Corinna murmured, 'you can't believe how much.'

There was an unbearable electricity between them, and with a muted groan he pushed her back against the pillows and began kissing her, and she returned his kisses like a starving man suddenly confronted with a plate of food. He buried his head against her neck and she caressed the dark hair.

'What did she hope to gain?' Corinna asked.

'Nothing and everything. She couldn't have me and the urge to destroy was the next best thing.' His hand cupped her breast and she gave a sigh of deep, exquisite longing.

'If it weren't for my father...' Antonio whispered shakily.

'He knew, didn't he?' The puzzle slotted together perfectly. Benjamin had requested her to return so that he could play his last, formidable trump.

'And I'm grateful to him,' Antonio said, parting her shirt, then her bra, to expose her breasts to his searching gaze. 'I want you, Corinna, and I love you. I need you to be with me, forever.'

She smiled, cradling his head. 'I love you,' she whispered. 'I've loved you for what seems like eternity. I'll live with you. If you get bored with me after three months...'

He rested his hand over her mouth. 'I could never get bored with you, my darling. Marry me and you'll see. I'll prove it. We'll go grey together. We'll sit in our rocking chairs together when we're eighty and I'll love every minute of it.'

He was staring at her intently, then he read the answer in her eyes and he smiled.

'Do you mean that?' she asked, and he nodded lazily.

'So sure that I would willingly shout it from the rooftops.' He stroked her body, from thigh to breast, his hand returning to slip under the lacy underwear, to caress that warm, wet place with a steady rhythm. 'But not yet,' he murmured. 'Right now, there are a few things I'd much rather be doing.'

And she laughed happily. She could think of a few herself. They were all part of paradise.

# THREE LOVE STORIES...

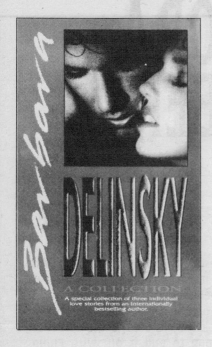

A beautiful collection of three individual love stories from *New York Times* bestselling author Barbara Delinsky – each featuring the charming and irrepressible matchmaker, Victoria Lesser.

A very collectable volume, offering new fans the chance to sample some of Delinsky's earlier works and for long-time fans to collect an edition to treasure.

## W**O**RLDWIDE

**AVAILABLE FROM SEPTEMBER     PRICED £4.99**

# Next Month's Romances

Each month you can choose from a wide variety of romance with Mills & Boon. Below are the new titles to look out for next month, why not ask either Mills & Boon Reader Service or your Newsagent to reserve you a copy of the titles you want to buy — just tick the titles you would like and either post to Reader Service or take it to any Newsagent and ask them to order your books.

| Please save me the following titles: | | Please tick | ✓ |
|---|---|---|---|
| A VERY STYLISH AFFAIR | Emma Darcy | | |
| ELEMENT OF RISK | Robyn Donald | | |
| TO HAVE AND TO HOLD | Sally Wentworth | | |
| BURDEN OF INNOCENCE | Patricia Wilson | | |
| LOVERS NOT FRIENDS | Helen Brooks | | |
| THREADS OF DESTINY | Sara Wood | | |
| INNOCENT DECEIVER | Lilian Peake | | |
| WHISPER OF SCANDAL | Kathryn Ross | | |
| CALYPSO'S ENCHANTMENT | Kate Walker | | |
| SAVING THE DEVIL | Sophie Weston | | |
| BETWEEN TWO LOVES | Rosemary Hammond | | |
| DREAM MAN | Quinn Wilder | | |
| STEP IN THE DARK | Marjorie Lewty | | |
| LOVESTORM | Jennifer Taylor | | |
| DECEPTIVE DESIRE | Sally Carr | | |
| A PASSIONATE DECEIT | Kate Proctor | | |

If you would like to order these books in addition to your regular subscription from Mills & Boon Reader Service please send £1.90 per title to: Mills & Boon Reader Service, Freepost, P.O. Box 236, Croydon, Surrey, CR9 9EL, quote your Subscriber No:................................... (if applicable) and complete the name and address details below. Alternatively, these books are available from many local Newsagents including W H Smith, J Menzies, Martins and other paperback stockists from 9 December 1994.

Name:.............................................................................

Address:..........................................................................

........................................................Post Code:.........................

**To Retailer: If you would like to stock M&B books please contact your regular book/magazine wholesaler for details.**

You may be mailed with offers from other reputable companies as a result of this application.
If you would rather not take advantage of these opportunities please tick box. ☐